a faraway island

a faraway island

ANNIKA THOR

Translated from the Swedish by Linda Schenck

Delacorte Press

Translation copyright © 2009 by Linda Schenck
Map illustration copyright © 2009 by Rick Britton

Delacorte Press is a registered trademark and the colophon is a trademark of Random House, Inc.

Visit us on the Web! www.randomhouse.com/kids

Educators and librarians, for a variety of teaching tools, visit us at www.randomhouse.com/teachers

Library of Congress Cataloging-in-Publication Data
Thor, Annika.
[En ö i havet. English]
A faraway island / Annika Thor ; translated from the Swedish by Linda Schenck.
p. cm.
Summary: In 1939 Sweden, two Jewish sisters wait for their parents to flee the Nazis in Austria, but while eight-year-old Nellie settles in quickly, twelve-year-old Stephie feels stranded at the end of the world, with a foster mother who is as cold and unforgiving as the island on which they live.
ISBN 978-0-385-73617-6 (hardcover) — ISBN 978-0-385-90590-9 (lib. bdg.) — ISBN 978-0-375-89370-4 (e-book)
1. World War, 1939–1945—Refugees—Juvenile fiction. [1. World War, 1939–1945— Refugees—Fiction. 2. Refugees—Fiction. 3. Sisters—Fiction. 4. Jews—Sweden—Fiction. 5. Islands—Fiction. 6. Sweden—History— 20th century—Fiction.] I. Schenck, Linda. II. Title.
PZ7.T3817Far 2009
[Fic]—dc22
2009015420

The text of this book is set in 12-point Goudy.

Book design by Kenny Holcomb

Printed in the United States of America

10 9 8 7 6 5 4 3 2 1

First American Edition

To Sara and Rebecka

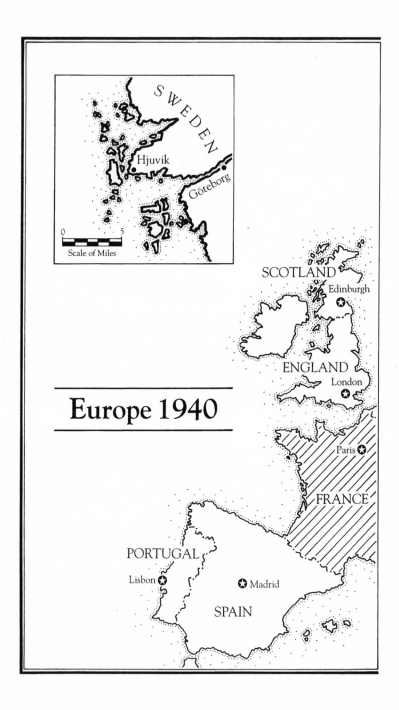

Europe 1940

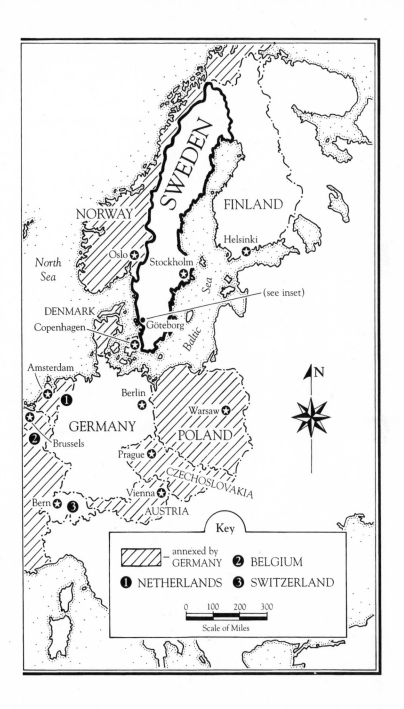

North
Sea

NORWAY

SWEDEN

FINLAND

Helsinki

Oslo

Stockholm

Baltic Sea

(see inset)

DENMARK

Copenhagen

Göteborg

Amsterdam

❶

Berlin

Warsaw

GERMANY

POLAND

❷

Brussels

Prague

CZECHOSLOVAKIA

Vienna

Bern

❸

AUSTRIA

N

Key

///// – annexed by GERMANY ❷ BELGIUM

❶ NETHERLANDS ❸ SWITZERLAND

0   100   200   300

Scale of Miles

one

The train slows to a halt. A voice over a loudspeaker shouts in an unknown language.

Stephie presses her nose to the window. Through the steam from the locomotive, she sees a sign and, farther down, a brick building with a glass roof.

"Are we there, Stephie?" Nellie asks anxiously. "Is this where we get off?"

"I'm not sure," Stephie answers, "but I think so."

She stands up on the seat to reach the luggage rack, lifting Nellie's suitcase down first, then her own. Their school knapsacks are on the floor at their feet. They must be sure not to leave anything on the train. This is all they were allowed to bring with them, and it is very little indeed.

A lady in a summer suit and hat appears in the doorway of their compartment. She addresses them in German.

"Hurry, hurry," she says. "This is Göteborg. Our destination."

The lady moves along to the next compartment without waiting for an answer.

Stephie pulls on her own knapsack, then helps her sister. "Take your suitcase!" she says.

"It's so heavy," Nellie complains, lifting it anyway. Hand in hand, they walk out into the train corridor. There are already a number of children gathered, all eager to disembark.

Soon the station platform is crowded with children and luggage. Behind them, the train pulls away, thudding and squealing. Some of the smaller children are crying. One little boy is calling for his mamma.

"Your mamma's not here," Stephie tells him. "She can't come to you. But you'll be getting a new mother here, one who's just as nice."

"Mamma, mamma," the little boy wails. The lady in the summer suit lifts him up and carries him.

"Come along," she says to the other children. "Follow me."

They walk behind her in a line like ducklings and enter the station, the building with the high, arched glass roof. A man with a big camera moves toward them. The sudden flash is blinding. One of the smaller children screams.

"Stop it, mister," the lady escorting them says curtly. "You're frightening the young ones."

The man goes on taking pictures anyway.

"This is my job, lady," he says. "Yours is to look after the poor little refugee children. Mine is to take the heartbreaking pictures so you'll get more money to do your work."

He takes a few more shots.

Stephie turns her face away. She doesn't want to be a refugee child in a heartbreaking picture in some magazine. She doesn't want to be someone people have to give money for.

The lady leads them to the far end of a large waiting area, part of which has been cordoned off and is full of grown-ups. An older woman with glasses moves toward them.

"Welcome to Sweden," she says. "We are so glad you got here safely. We represent the local relief committee. You'll be safe here until you can be reunited with your parents."

This lady speaks German, too, but with a funny accent.

A younger woman takes out a list and begins calling names: "Ruth Baumann . . . Stephan Fischer . . . Eva Goldberg . . ."

Every time she calls a name, a child raises his or her hand, then walks over to the lady with the list. The lady double-checks the name against the brown name tags that the child, like all the other children, has hanging from his or her neck. One of the adults who've been waiting steps forward, takes the child, and departs. The children who are too small to respond to the roll call are pointed out and collected from their bench.

The list is in alphabetical order, so Stephie realizes she and Nellie will have a long wait. Her stomach is aching with hunger, and her whole body longs for a bed to stretch out on. The crowded railway compartment has been their home since early yesterday morning. The miles and miles of track have carried them all the way from Vienna, Austria, far from Mamma and Papa. The rails were a link between them. Now the girls have been cut off. They're all alone.

3

Slowly the groups of children and adults begin to dwindle. Nellie cuddles up to Stephie.

"When will it be our turn, Stephie? Isn't there anybody here for us?"

"They haven't come to S yet," Stephie explains. "We have to wait."

"I'm so hungry," Nellie whines. "And so tired. And so very hungry."

"There's nothing left to eat," Stephie informs her. "We finished our sandwiches ages ago. You'll have to be patient until we get to where we're going. Sit down on your suitcase if you're too tired to stand."

Nellie sits down on her little case, chin in hands. Her long black braids reach nearly to the floor.

"Nellie, I'll bet we're going to be living in a real palace," Stephie says, trying to comfort her sister. "With zillions of rooms. And a view of the sea."

"Will I have my own bedroom?" Nellie asks.

"Sure," Stephie promises.

"Oh, no," Nellie moans. "I'd rather share with you."

"Eleonore Steiner," Stephie hears the lady call out.

"That's you! Say 'Here,' " Stephie whispers.

"Eleonore Steiner," the lady with the list repeats. "Come forward!"

Stephie pulls Nellie along, zigzagging between pieces of luggage. "We're here," she says.

The lady looks back down at her list. "Stephanie Steiner?" she asks.

Stephie nods.

"Steiner," the lady repeats loudly. "Eleonore and Stephanie Steiner!"

No grown-up comes forward.

"Stephie," asks Nellie, her voice trembling, "doesn't anybody want us?"

Stephie doesn't answer, just clutches Nellie's hand tightly. The lady with the list turns to her.

"You'll have to wait a bit longer," she says, moving the two sisters to the side. "If you'll just stand here, I'll be back shortly."

The older woman takes over the roll call. After a while, all the other children are gone. Stephie and Nellie are alone with their suitcases.

"Can we go home now?" asks Nellie. "Back to Mamma and Papa?"

Stephie shakes her head. Nellie begins to cry.

"Shhh," Stephie hisses. "Don't start blubbering, now. You're not a crybaby, are you?"

Heels clatter against the marble floor. Footsteps approach. The younger woman quickly explains something to the older one. She takes a pen out of her bag and writes on Stephie and Nellie's name tags: *These children do not speak Swedish.*

"Come along," she says to Stephie. "I'm going to take you to the boat."

Stephie takes her suitcase in one hand and Nellie by the other. Silently, they follow the lady out of the station.

two

The sun is bright, the August heat oppressive, as Stephie, Nellie, and the lady from the relief committee clamber into a taxicab outside the train station. Stephie is all itchy inside her heavy new coat. Before they left for Sweden, their mother had a winter coat made for each of them by Fräulein Gerlach, the seamstress. Mamma asked Fräulein Gerlach for especially thick linings; she knew Sweden was a cold country.

The coats are light blue with dark blue velvet collars. Their matching hats are blue velvet, too. Stephie would have loved the coat if it hadn't been made because they were leaving.

After a long ride the taxi stops at the harbor and they get out. Ships as large as buildings are docked along the pier.

A little white steamer out at the far end resembles a toy boat as it bobs in the waves.

The lady pays the taxi driver and walks ahead of Stephie, holding Nellie by one hand and Nellie's suitcase in the other. Stephie drags her own heavy suitcase behind.

When they get to the gangway, the woman buys tickets from one of the crew members. She speaks to him in Swedish, pointing to the girls. At first the man shakes his head, but the woman continues talking until, finally, he nods.

"Come on," he says to the girls, showing them to two seats in the covered section of the boat. Nellie looks disappointed.

"I want to stand out there," Nellie says to Stephie, pointing to the deck. "Ask him if it's all right."

"You ask!" says Stephie.

Nellie shrugs and sits down. When the engines begin to throb, Stephie realizes they never said goodbye to the lady from the relief committee, and she hurries to the aft deck. The lady is gone.

The boat pulls away from the pier and out to the middle of the river. Black smoke rises from the smokestack, dissolving into thin mist.

Nellie stays in her seat, looking as pitiful as a rag doll. Stephie notices that her sister's coat is buttoned crooked, and that one of her cheeks has a smudge of dirt on it. She rubs at the smudge with her handkerchief.

"Where's this boat taking us?" Nellie asks.

"We'll soon see," Stephie replies.

"To the bathing resort on the coast?"

"Sure."

"Tell me what it's like," Nellie requests.

"There are long, soft, sandy beaches," Stephie tells her, "and palm trees growing along the boardwalk. People lie on deck chairs under colorful beach umbrellas. The children play in the water and build sand castles. There are ice cream vendors, carrying freezer boxes around their necks."

Stephie's never been to the seaside. But Evi, her best friend in Vienna, was at an Italian resort two years ago. Afterward, she told Stephie all about the beach and the palm trees, the beach chairs and the ice cream vendors. Stephie and Nellie and their mother and father always spent their summer vacations at a little country hotel on the shores of the Danube River. Or at least they used to, before the Nazis came along.

Stephie senses they're being stared at. She looks up to find two old men, on the bench opposite the girls, gazing openly and curiously at them.

"Why are they looking at us like that?" Nellie asks anxiously.

"It's the name tags," Stephie guesses.

One of the men puts a wad of snuff under his top lip. A drop of brown saliva seeps out of the corner of his mouth. He says something to his friend, chuckling.

"Let's take them off," Stephie decides, folding the name tags into her knapsack. "Come on, we're going outside."

The girls stand on the deck. They can see where the river joins the ocean. A tugboat is piloting one of the big ships toward the port. The little one seems to be pulling the big one, like a child eagerly tugging at its mother to show her something. It looks funny. Red brick warehouses line the riverbanks. Huge loading cranes jut into the air, looking like giraffes with long necks.

Nellie fingers her coral necklace. It's actually her mother's, bought by Papa long, long ago when the two honeymooned in Italy. Nellie has always loved the irregular slivers of pink coral. Her mother gave it to her just as they were leaving on this journey.

"Tell me more about the resort, Stephie," she begs. "Will I be able to swim there?"

"You'll have to learn," says Stephie. "Every afternoon the people go to their hotel rooms for a rest. After dinner they stroll in the park and listen to the band."

"Are we going to stay at a hotel?"

"I don't know. Maybe the people who are taking us in will be hotel owners."

"Then we'll get everything, free of charge."

"Or maybe they have a house at the shore. With a private beach."

"Will they have children?"

Stephie shrugs. "I hope they have a dog," she says.

"Will there be a piano?" Nellie asks for the hundredth time.

"Of course there will," Stephie assures her.

Stephie knows how badly Nellie misses their piano. She had just started lessons when they had to move out of their spacious apartment by the park with the huge Ferris wheel. If it had been up to Mamma, they would have taken the piano with them, despite the fact that it would nearly have filled up the entire single room they were forced to move into. But Papa refused.

"There's barely space for four beds as it is," he said. "Do you think we could sleep on the piano?"

The boat has left the river now and is out on the open sea. They pass rocky cliffs and lots of little islets. It's windier out here, and dark clouds are gathering at the horizon. Nellie tugs at her sister's coat sleeve.

"Stephie, will there really be one? Are you sure?"

"What?"

"A piano I can play," says Nellie. "Will there?"

"Yes, yes," Stephie promises her. "But do stop nagging!"

Nellie starts humming a children's song, one of the melodies she knows on the piano. Nellie has their mother's beautiful voice, while Stephie can hardly carry a tune.

The boat passes a peninsula. The wind hits, and the boat starts to rock. Stephie hangs on to the rail.

"I'm cold," Nellie says.

"Go on inside, then."

Nellie hesitates. "Aren't you coming?"

"Not yet," says Stephie. The deck has begun to roll under her feet. She's feeling queasy. The sky is getting darker and thunder roars from afar. Nellie heads for the cabin, then changes her mind and comes back.

"Go on in," says Stephie. "I won't be long."

She clings to the rail, eyes shut tight. The boat rocks from side to side. Stephie cranes over the water and vomits. Her throat is burning and she feels exhausted and dizzy.

"Are you ill, Stephie?" Nellie asks nervously.

"Seasick," says Stephie. "I suppose I'm seasick."

She hangs on tightly to the rail, eyes still shut. Her knees are weak under her. Nellie helps her back to the cabin. She lies down on a bench, using her knapsack as a pillow, and rests. The world is spinning. . . .

◇ ◇ ◇

From the depths of sleep, Stephie feels someone tugging at her sleeve.

"Leave me alone," she mumbles. "I need to sleep."

But the tugging persists. She cannot ignore it. Her eyes open.

"Stephie!" Nellie shouts. "We're there."

It takes Stephie a moment to remember. Nellie is standing next to her, hopping up and down eagerly. Her cheeks are rosy and the ribbon on one of her braids has come undone.

"Hurry up! We're there."

three

When Stephie steps out onto the deck, the odor hits her like an invisible wall.

The air reeks of salt and fish and something rotten. Nauseous again, Stephie swallows hard and looks around.

The boat has pulled up alongside a wooden dock lined with white fishing boats that have broad hulls and short masts. The wind rattles their rigging. All kinds of little boats are moored along the jetties. A breakwater of huge boulders shelters this small harbor from the waves.

Tall wooden racks line the harbor. Some of them are empty; some have fishnets hanging to dry. One is covered with triangular shapes that look like white bats, their wings spread wide.

The dock itself is dotted with red-and-gray boathouses,

opening toward the water. Behind them are low houses, painted in pastel shades. They look as if they're springing right up out of the rocks.

Before anyone can disembark, lots of crates and sacks have to be unloaded. A boy with a rubber-wheeled barrow rolls them out onto the dock. A sack breaks, and some potatoes go tumbling into the water. Nellie laughs, but is soon silenced when she sees how a big red-faced man scolds the boy.

At last it's their turn. Stephie holds Nellie tightly by the hand as they walk down the gangway.

A woman is waiting for them on the dock. She's wearing a knitted cardigan over her flowered dress, and she has a polka-dotted scarf tied around her head. A few strands of fair hair have escaped at her temples. As soon as she sees the girls, her face lights up.

"Eleonore . . . Stephanie," she says, pronouncing their names very strangely. She bends down, embracing Nellie and kissing her on the cheek.

"How do you do?" Stephie says, extending a hand. "My name is Stephie."

The woman takes Stephie's hand, saying a few words in the unfamiliar language.

"What did she say?" Nellie asks.

"I don't really know," says Stephie. "It must have been Swedish."

"Doesn't she speak German?" Nellie wonders. "Can't she understand us?" Her voice trembles.

Stephie shakes her head. "We're going to have to learn Swedish."

"Stephie?" The woman asks. "Ah, Stephanie—Stephie?"

"*Ja,*" says Stephie. "Stephanie—Stephie." She points to her little sister. "Eleonore—Nellie."

The woman smiles, nodding. "Alma," she says. "Alma Lindberg. Auntie Alma. Come along!"

Alma has a bicycle propped up against one of the boat-houses. She ties Nellie's suitcase to the carrier and, taking Nellie by the hand, walks her bicycle along the narrow road between the houses. Stephie follows, carrying her suitcase.

The houses are very close together. They seem to creep along the ground, clinging to the slope for dear life. Each one has its own little yard with low bushes and gnarled fruit trees. The houses by the harbor are all small and low, but as the three proceed along the road, the houses become larger.

Auntie Alma walks fast, with long, determined strides. Nellie practically has to run to keep up. Stephie finds herself lagging farther and farther behind. Her throat is dry; she has a terrible, sour taste in her mouth. Although she's already thousands of miles from home, she now has the impression that every step she takes is moving her far from the buildings, streets, and people she knows.

Stephie's suitcase feels as heavy as lead. She sets it on the ground and drags it behind her for a while, then tries shoving it in front of her, kicking it along with one foot.

The sound of the suitcase on the gravel makes Auntie Alma turn around. She stops, piles Stephie's case onto her bicycle seat, and shows Stephie how to walk alongside holding one hand on it to keep it steady. It's not easy, but much better than having to carry it.

"Stephie," Nellie whines, "where are the sandy beaches? Where's the bandstand?"

Stephie ignores her sister's questions.

"What if there's no hotel? And no palm trees, and no dog, and no piano?" Nellie goes on, her voice tense and anxious.

"Shush now," Stephie hisses impatiently. "We're not there yet."

At that very moment they stop outside a yellow wooden house with a glass-enclosed veranda. The flower beds on either side of the doorway are full of bright flowers, red, yellow, and blue. Two blond-headed children rush out the door and into Auntie Alma's arms.

"They have children!" says Nellie, her voice happy. "And they're younger than me!"

Stephie and Nellie leave their coats and suitcases in the vestibule and go into the kitchen. At the table sits a woman with a thin, stern-looking face. Her salt-and-pepper hair is twisted into a tight bun at the nape of her neck. Her pale eyes inspect Stephie and Nellie from head to toe.

"What scrawny little things," the woman says to Auntie Alma. "Pitifully thin. Let us hope we can make something of them."

"Aunt Märta," Auntie Alma says, gesturing toward the older woman. Stephie shakes her hand and curtseys. Aunt Märta's hand is cold and rough.

Auntie Alma places a big platter of sticky buns on the kitchen table. She pours four glasses of black currant juice, as well as coffee for herself and Aunt Märta.

"*Bulle*," Auntie Alma says in Swedish, indicating the buns, once all four of them are seated around the table. She goes on to tell Stephie and Nellie the words for glass, table, stool, and cup in this new language.

Stephie and Nellie try to imitate the strange words. Some are similar to the German words for the same objects, others very different.

"*Stol, Stuhl.*" Stephie says the Swedish word first, then the German one. Auntie Alma imitates her, trying to get the German word right. "*Schtol,*" it comes out. Auntie Alma laughs at herself.

"*Schtol, schtol,*" her children parrot with pleasure. Then they point to themselves, shouting: "Elsa!" "John!" "Elsa!" "John!"

By the time Aunt Märta gets up from the table, Nellie and Stephie know ten words of Swedish. When Aunt Märta comes back into the kitchen, she is carrying Stephie's coat. She extends it to her.

"Stephie?" Nellie asks anxiously. "What's happening? What does she mean?"

"I'm not sure," Stephie answers. Slowly she puts on her coat and buttons it all the way up. Auntie Alma and the children walk her and Aunt Märta to the door.

"Are you leaving me here, Stephie?" Nellie whispers. "Why can't you stay?"

Aunt Märta walks out the door. Stephie picks up her knapsack and puts it on again.

"Don't leave me!" Nellie pleads. "I don't want to stay here without you!"

"Don't make a fuss," says Stephie. "We have to do as we're told."

"But Mamma promised we'd live together. She said so."

"I know. Maybe this is just for tonight. Don't be afraid."

Nellie hugs Stephie tight. "Will you be here in the morning?" she asks, sounding very small.

"Of course I will," says Stephie, not knowing whether she'll be able to keep that promise. She walks through the door behind Aunt Märta.

Stephie turns around once she's down the steps. Auntie Alma is in the doorway with Nellie, a protective arm around her shoulders.

Aunt Märta leads her bicycle out through the gate. Once they're on the road, she pats the carrier. Stephie climbs up, and Aunt Märta sets her suitcase on her lap. Aunt Märta gets on the seat and starts pedaling.

Stephie's never ridden a bicycle. Never had a ride on one, either. Her mother would never allow her to bike on the streets of Vienna, with all those cars and trams. Now she has to balance herself with one hand, holding tightly to the carrier, and balance her suitcase with the other. Every time they hit a bump or a stone, Stephie fears the whole assemblage will veer off its equilibrium and she'll tumble.

The farther out along the island road they get, the fewer and farther between the houses are. They pass through a thicket of trees and bushes. The road twists and turns among bare gray rocks. Pale purple heather blooms in the crevices.

Aunt Märta pedals slowly up a long hill and stops at the crest. In front of them is the endless, leaden-gray ocean.

The dark clouds form a ceiling over the water. Gray-brown cliffs and rocks extend along the edge of the ocean. The waves break on the cliffs, tossing showers of white spray. In the distance, just barely visible, there's the brown silhouette of a sail against the backdrop of sea and sky. After that there's nothing but the horizon, a thin ribbon of light at the far edge.

The end of the world, Stephie thinks. *This must be the end of the world.*

The road winds down to an isolated house, pressed up close to a stony cliff, as if seeking protection from the wind. There's a red boathouse, too, down at the water's edge. A boat is bobbing in the water, by a dock.

Thunder rumbles softly in the distance. A blinding streak of lightning illuminates the dark sky. Aunt Märta points down at the house and says something. Although Stephie doesn't understand the words, she realizes that this is where she is going to be living. Way out at the end of the world.

four

The first drops of rain strike Stephie's forehead as the bicycle rolls down the hill toward the house. The road ends at a gate. From the top of the hill the house looked tiny. Now Stephie sees that it's two stories high, built upon a tall stone foundation. Steps leading up to the front door are flanked by windows that appear to be staring at Stephie. The house looks stern, with straight lines, flat surfaces, and no frills.

Aunt Märta props her bicycle against the house and walks up the steps, ahead of Stephie.

Back in Vienna, when Stephie opened the door to their apartment, she would catch whiffs of Papa's cigars and Mamma's perfume. After they moved and had only the single room, plus a kitchen they shared with three other families, there were always the smells of boiled cabbage and baby diapers. Every home has its own special odor. Auntie Alma's

19

house smelled of fresh bread. Here, Stephie's nose takes in the sting of cleaning fluid.

Aunt Märta shows her around the house. In the kitchen everything is neat and tidy. There is an old wood-burning stove with a hood, as well as a modern electric range. The front room has rough wooden furniture. One corner is occupied by a big rocking chair. On top of a table covered with a thick, embroidered tablecloth is an enormous book. Presumably a Bible. There are blue-striped cotton curtains on the windows.

At the top of the stairs is a bay window under the gable, and a little niche with a bench. This is a spot Stephie instantly likes: light but still cozy, a place to sit and read, or just look out the window. Through an open door she glimpses a room with two beds.

Aunt Märta leads Stephie into a little room under the eaves, with a sloping ceiling. The drab, brown-patterned wallpaper makes the room feel even smaller than it is. At the far end is a tiny square window, barely large enough to let in any light. Under it are a table and a plain rib-backed wooden chair. Along the longer wall stands a bed with a crocheted spread, and on the other side of the door is a brown dresser with three drawers. That's all. No decorations or bric-a-brac, no books, no art.

Unless, of course, you count the framed picture on the wall above the chest of drawers. It's of a man with long hair and a beard, wearing a pink robe that touches the ground. He's holding out his arms in a gesture of benediction. Behind him, wide rays of light extend from an invisible source.

That's Jesus, Stephie thinks. *Why would Aunt Märta put a picture of Jesus in my room? Doesn't she know I'm Jewish?*

Aunt Märta sets Stephie's suitcase on the table and opens it. Obediently, Stephie begins to unpack. Aunt Märta shows her a curtained-off area on the landing where she's supposed to hang her dresses. Behind a second curtain is a little table with a washbasin and a towel.

Stephie puts her stockings and underwear in the top dresser drawer, her sweaters and blouses in the next. In the bottom one she puts her books, her diary, her stationery and pens, and her jewelry box. She lays her scruffy teddy bear on the bed. Although it's been years since she cuddled her bear at night, she couldn't leave him behind.

She places her photos on the dresser. Separate portraits of her parents, and a picture of the whole family together on an outing to the Wienerwald park. Her papa is sitting on a log; Stephie is on the ground, leaning against his legs; Nellie is playing horsey, straddling the log; Mamma is standing behind Papa, her hands on his shoulders. She's leaning forward a little, as if she's about to whisper something in his ear.

The picture is two years old. In those days, the Steiners were still an ordinary family, taking the streetcar, going to movies and concerts, enjoying vacations. But less than a year after the picture was taken, the Nazis invaded Austria, annexing the country to Germany. Things the Steiner family had always taken for granted were suddenly prohibited. Forbidden to all people like them, to Jews.

Stephie sinks down onto the bed. Her head is pounding

from exhaustion. She longs to sleep, and finds herself unable to get up off the bed until Aunt Märta returns to open each of the dresser drawers and scrutinize the contents. Aunt Märta takes out one or two garments and refolds them even more neatly.

When Stephie stands up, Aunt Märta smoothes out the bedspread, removing every wrinkle and crease. She signals to Stephie to follow her and goes back downstairs. Stephie walks slowly behind her, feeling as if she is entering unknown territory.

The table in the kitchen is set for two. Aunt Märta puts out their dinner: a steaming bowl of boiled potatoes and a serving platter with two fried fish on it. Whole fish, with the heads still on.

When they are seated, Aunt Märta clasps her hands and says a few soft words. After placing one of the fish on Stephie's plate, she passes her the potatoes.

Stephie stares at the fish, and it stares right back at her with its dead, white eye. Aunt Märta cuts the head off hers and uses her knife to remove the skin. Stephie watches and imitates. The fish head is parted from the body with a horrid crack.

Aunt Märta pours two glasses of milk and hands Stephie a bowl of red preserves. Back home, they had jam with their pancakes, and sometimes raspberry jam in their tea. Papa always said his mother, who was born in Russia, drank her tea with a spoonful of jam in it. But jam with fish? Stephie takes a spoonful and puts it on her plate. To her relief, she sees Aunt Märta do so as well.

She pokes at the fish with her fork, then puts a tiny bite

in her mouth and takes a deep drink of milk, swallowing as fast as she can. The milk masks the fishy taste.

If only she didn't have that sickening fish head on her plate! She tries not to look at it. But pretending it isn't there only earns her a mouthful of bones in her next bite. The bones stick in her throat.

She's nearly emptied her glass. Does she dare ask for more milk? And what should she say?

She drinks up the last drop and points to the pitcher.

"*Bitte,*" she says. The German word for "please."

Aunt Märta nods and pours her another glass. Stephie chews and swallows, chews and swallows. She hides as much of the fish as she can under the pile of skin and bones on her plate. Once again her milk glass is empty. She can't possibly ask for even more, and can just barely get the last bite of fish to go down.

Aunt Märta's finished eating. She gets up from the table, takes a pot of hot water from the stove, and pours it into the sink. Then she points to the plates and to the sink filled with water.

In the days when they lived in their own large apartment, Stephie's family had a cook, a housemaid, and a cleaning lady who came once a week. After they moved, Mamma did all the housework herself. Papa thought Stephie and Nellie should help with simpler tasks like the dishes and dusting. But Mamma refused.

"My daughters are never going to be household slaves," she told him.

Well, she should see Stephie now, awkwardly scraping the remains of the fish from the plates down into the slop pail. One at a time, Stephie slides the plates into the hot water. Finding the dishcloth, she washes away the fatty remains; then she rinses each plate in fresh water.

By the time Stephie has cleaned up after the meal, her hands are swollen and red. She wipes the table and rinses the dishcloth under the cold-water tap. The dishcloth has a sour smell.

Aunt Märta sweeps the floor and wipes the stove. She inspects each plate and, pointing with one finger, shows Stephie where she hasn't done a good job on one of them.

When they're finished, Aunt Märta unties her apron, turns on the radio in the front room, and settles into the rocking chair. Stephie finds herself standing in the kitchen. If there had been music on the radio she would have gone in and listened. But it's just the voice of a man speaking words she cannot understand. Aunt Märta doesn't seem bothered about her right now, so Stephie decides to go up to her room.

five

Stephie tiptoes quietly up the stairs and into the little room under the eaves. She opens the bottom dresser drawer and removes her stationery and her fountain pen. The pen is new, a gift from her father on her last evening at home.

"So that you can write us beautiful letters," he said as he lifted it out of the little box lined in dark blue velvet.

Stephie takes a sheet of writing paper, along with the pen, and settles herself in at the bay window. She unscrews the cap on the pen and looks out at the landscape.

Rain clatters against the windowpane. The wind is gusty, but she can see the stony slope that leads down to the water. Patches of grass sprout up here and there, as do a few gnarled juniper bushes. The water's edge is marked by a rocky shore, stones and pebbles as far as the eye can see.

Waves are crashing against the shore so loudly that Stephie can hear them through the closed window. Everything in sight is gray—gray stones, a gray ocean, a gray sky.

Dearest Mamma and Papa, she writes. *I miss you so. We have now arrived at the place where we will be staying. It's a far-away island. We came out by boat, but I don't know how long the ride took as I was seasick and then I fell asleep.*

Nellie and I weren't put in the same family. I don't know why. Nellie's living with Auntie Alma. She's nice and has two little children of her own. I'm at Aunt Märta's house. She's . . .

Stephie stops, her pen resting on the paper. How to describe Aunt Märta? She imagines the woman's stern face, her tightly pulled-back knot of hair, the sharp lines around her mouth, and eyes so pale gray they appear almost colorless.

Fish eyes, Stephie thinks with a little shiver.

. . . quite strict, she writes. *She doesn't speak German. Neither does Auntie Alma. I'm not sure Nellie and I will have anyone but each other to talk to.*

Something wet strikes the paper, dissolving the last word into a puddle.

Mamma! she writes. *Oh, Mamma, please come and get us. This place is nothing but sea and stones. I can't live here. If you don't come and get me, I think I'm going to die.*

Stephie pushes the letter aside. Her throat aches with held-back tears. She runs into the little room and is about to throw herself onto the bed when she remembers that she mustn't wrinkle the bedspread. Instead she sinks to the floor, resting her head against the edge of the bed.

When she finally stops sobbing, Stephie feels emptied out, as if she had nothing inside but a gaping hole. She goes out to the little washstand on the landing and rinses her face with cold water.

Her letter is still on the windowsill. Stephie picks it up and reads through it. . . . *come and get us.* What was she thinking? Mamma and Papa don't have entry visas for Sweden. They couldn't come if they wanted to.

She can't send a letter like that home. Mamma would be distraught. She might even regret having allowed them to leave. Papa would be disappointed in Stephie, his "big girl."

With great determination Stephie crumples the letter into a hard ball. She looks for a wastepaper basket, but doesn't find one anywhere. By the window in her room is a little vent with a pull-string attached. She tugs the string, opens the vent, and stuffs her ball of paper in. Then she sits down at the writing table with a fresh piece of paper in front of her, and starts a new letter.

Dearest Mamma and Papa!
We have now arrived at the place where we will be staying. It's an island in the sea. We came out by boat, which was very exciting. I have a second-floor room with a view of the sea. Everyone is very kind. We've already learned a little Swedish. It's not very hard.
I hope you will soon be getting your entry visas for America. Then all four of us will be together again. But until that day, you needn't worry about Nellie and me. We are fine here, and there is even a dog. It's brown and

27

white, and we are allowed to play with it all the time. I will write again soon and tell you more.

Your daughter,
Stephie

She writes the address on the envelope, folds the letter, and slips it in. She licks the flap and presses the envelope closed. Now all she needs is a stamp.

Aunt Märta is sitting at the kitchen table with a cup of coffee. Stephie shows her the letter.

"A stamp," she tries to say. "I need a stamp."

She points to the top right-hand corner of the envelope. Aunt Märta nods and says something. Stephie thinks she recognizes the word "post." Maybe they will have to go to the post office for stamps. Probably.

"Coffee?" Aunt Märta asks, pointing to her own cup. Stephie shakes her head. Coffee is for grown-ups. Aunt Märta goes to the larder and brings out the pitcher of milk. She holds it in one hand and pretends to lift a glass to her lips with the other. Stephie nods and smiles. Aunt Märta looks kind of funny when she tries to talk to her.

We're like two deaf-mutes, Stephie thinks. *Deaf-mutes who can't communicate in any language.*

Aunt Märta gives Stephie a glass of milk, and Stephie drinks it to the last drop. Then Aunt Märta puts the palms of her hands together, leans her cheek on her hands, and shuts her eyes. Stephie nods again. She's very tired now.

"Good night," she says, going upstairs.

She changes into her long flannel nightgown, washes, and brushes her teeth. She folds the bedspread very carefully, then hangs it over the foot of the bed. Her clothes are neatly folded on the chair.

It feels wonderful to slide under the covers, in spite of their unfamiliar smell. She buries her nose in her old teddy bear, feeling safe in the familiar scent of his fur. It smells like home.

Although she is exhausted, Stephie cannot fall asleep. She lies awake for ages, listening to the patter of the rain on the roof. She's never heard the rain so clearly from indoors before. A while later she tiptoes from the bed to look out the window. It's pitch black outside. Not so much as a streetlight.

"When you're twelve you'll have a bedroom of your own," her parents used to tell her when they were still living in their apartment. In those days she looked forward to not having to share the nursery with Nellie. Now she is twelve and has a room of her own. But in the wrong house. In the wrong country.

Finally her body begins to feel heavy. Stephie climbs back into bed and begins drifting off. She's nearly asleep when the door opens just a crack. Eyes closed, she hears footsteps approaching her bed. Lightly, as if in a dream, a hand brushes her cheek. A moment later, the door shuts again.

six

Stephie senses something is wrong even before her brain is awake enough to remember what. She presses her eyes tight shut, trying to stay asleep. But she can't.

Sunlight trickles through the crack between the curtains. She can hear footsteps and clatter from the kitchen. It's morning, her first morning on the island. The first of how many?

"Six months at the very most," her father had said on the platform at the Vienna railway station. "In just a few months, no more than six, we'll have our entry visas. Then we'll meet up in Amsterdam and travel to America together."

Stephie turns her head to look at the photos on the dresser. Her mother is smiling, her father is looking gravely at her from behind his glasses. She sits up in bed, pulling her knees to her chest.

"No need to worry, Mamma and Papa," she says aloud. "I'm a big girl now. I'm taking good care of Nellie."

Stephie gets dressed, washes her face and hands, and combs her hair in front of the mirror over the little wash-basin. Her hair is very tangled and takes time to comb through; she hasn't combed it properly since the morning they left for the station in Vienna two full days ago.

When Stephie or Nellie complained about the difficulty of having long hair, their mother always used to tell them it was worth the trouble.

"When a person has such lovely, thick hair, it's a shame to cut it short."

Stephanie stares at her reflection, and the girl in the mirror stares back. The face she sees is thin, with brown eyes and wide lips. Her dark hair hangs almost all the way to her waist. She parts it down the middle and plaits it into neat braids.

◊　◊　◊

"Good morning," she greets Aunt Märta in German as she enters the kitchen. Aunt Märta's Swedish reply sounds almost the same.

For breakfast there's oatmeal and milk. The oatmeal is thick and gluey, but Stephie's hungry enough to gobble it all down. Aunt Märta, looking pleased, dishes up a second helping.

While Stephie is eating, the telephone rings. Aunt Märta answers and has quite a long conversation. After she hangs up, she turns to Stephie.

"Nellie," she says, pointing out the kitchen window. "You . . . Nellie."

Stephie's spoon clatters into her bowl. Has something happened to Nellie? Is she sick? Has she had an accident? Stammering, she tries to ask what's wrong. But Aunt Märta doesn't understand. She follows Stephie out the door and points to her bicycle.

Maybe it isn't so hard to ride a bike after all. Stephie wheels the bike out to the road and puts a foot down on one of the pedals. But as soon as she lifts her other foot, she loses her balance and has to put it right back onto the ground. She tries several times. On the fourth try she manages to push the pedals around once before falling over. The bicycle comes down on top of her and one of her knees is scraped so badly it's bleeding. She gives up and leans the bicycle back against the house.

She runs up the hill, along the rocky path, and through the little thicket. It's much farther than it seemed yesterday, when she was sitting on Aunt Märta's carrier. Breathless, a pain piercing her side, she reaches the yellow frame house and pounds on the door.

Auntie Alma opens, takes her by the hand, and draws her inside. Nellie, still in her nightgown, eyes red from crying, is at the kitchen table. The moment she catches sight of Stephie she throws herself into her arms.

"Stephie, Stephie," she sobs, "I want to go home! I want my mamma!"

"What on earth is wrong?" Stephie asks sharply.

Nellie just cries harder.

"Take care of Nellie," her mother had said when they were leaving. "Comfort her when she is unhappy and frightened. You're the big one."

"Did something happen?" Stephie asks her, forcing a kindly tone into her voice.

Nellie nods mutely.

"What?"

"I couldn't help it," Nellie whispers.

"Tell me."

"I wet my bed."

"What?" Stephie says again in alarm. Nellie stopped wetting her bed five years back.

"I just couldn't hold it. I tried but I had to pee so badly."

"In your sleep?"

Nellie shakes her head.

"You were awake? So why didn't you go to the toilet?"

"There is no toilet," Nellie explains. "You have to go outside, to a special place in the backyard. A smelly little building."

"Was that what stopped you from going?"

Nellie shakes her head again. "No, it wasn't that," she mumbles.

"What was it, then?"

"I didn't dare. It was so dark out, and I was scared they would come and take me away."

"Who?" Stephie asks, although she already knows.

"The police," Nellie whispers even more softly. "The Nazis."

"Nellie, we're in Sweden now," Stephie assures her. "There are no Nazis here. The police in this country don't come and take people away during the night. Don't you understand? That's why Mamma and Papa sent us here."

"I know that," says Nellie. "But in the dark, I forgot."

It takes a long time for Stephie to make it clear to Auntie Alma that Nellie is afraid to go to the outhouse in the dark. Eventually, though, she succeeds, and Auntie Alma puts a china chamber pot under Nellie's bed. Then she cleans Stephie's scraped knee with something that stings, and puts a bandage on it.

In the meantime Nellie has put her clothes on and clasped the coral necklace around her neck. Auntie Alma shakes her head, unclasps the necklace, and puts it in Nellie's dresser drawer. Nellie looks as if she's going to burst into tears again, until Auntie Alma pulls out her nicest dress, showing her that the necklace and the dress go together. Nellie should wear her necklace only when she's dressed up.

◊　◊　◊

The sky is blue now, the weather pleasant. Stephie and Nellie go out into the yard with Auntie Alma's children. Elsa and Nellie start playing with a baby doll at a table. They bathe her and dress and undress her, over and over again. John has a ball, and he motions to Stephie to throw it to him. He never manages to catch it on the fly.

A group of girls Stephie's age bike past, bathing suits flapping from their handlebars, towels clamped under their carriers.

They stop outside the fence, staring at Stephie and Nellie. One of them, tall and blond, says something to the others. They all laugh.

As if we were monkeys in the zoo, Stephie thinks.

"What do they want, Stephie?" Nellie asks uneasily. "Are they going to hurt us?"

"Oh, no," Stephie says in her firmest voice. "They're silly but they mean no harm."

A girl with bright red hair speaks to Stephie, who shakes her head to show she doesn't understand. The girl giggles. There's no ill will in her laugh.

The blond girl pedals off; the others follow. They bike in a group down the hill, bathing suits blowing in the wind.

"They must be on their way to the beach," says Nellie. "To swim. I want to go swimming, too."

"We can't," Stephie says in her sensible, big-sister voice. "We haven't got bathing suits."

For a long time they hadn't been allowed to go to the beach in Vienna. Not since signs prohibited them, signs that read JEWS FORBIDDEN. When Mamma was helping them pack, she had pulled out their old bathing suits, but it was clear they had outgrown them.

Aunt Märta arrives on her bicycle, a big bag dangling from her handlebars. Holding Stephie's letter, she points toward the village.

The post office, Stephie thinks, and decides to go along. She needs to see with her own eyes when her letter is mailed, to feel confident it is on its way.

"Wait here for me," she says to Nellie. "I'm going to the post office. I'll be right back."

The post office and the village shop are in the same building, a big, rectangular, flat-roofed structure. Stephie stands next to Aunt Märta, watching her buy a stamp from the lady at the window.

"It's for Vienna," Aunt Märta says. "Vienna, Austria."

"The German Reich," the lady corrects her. "Here you are, Mrs. Jansson. I didn't know you had friends abroad."

"The letter's from this girl," Aunt Märta explains. "She's sending it to her parents."

"And who is she, precisely?" the lady asks.

"A young Jewess," Aunt Märta tells her. "There's trouble in that part of the world, so Evert and I agreed to take her in. Until her parents can leave the country. I understand they're hoping to emigrate to America."

The post office lady sighs. "Poor little thing. All alone in the world."

"She's better off here than there," Aunt Märta says brusquely. "Her sister's here, too, you know."

"Oh me, oh my," the lady responds. "What terrible times we're living in. Do you think there'll be a war, Mrs. Jansson?"

"Man proposes and God disposes," Aunt Märta concludes, paying for the stamp with a coin from her wallet. "Thank you very much."

Stephie goes into the store with her, too, waiting while she shops. She recognizes the man behind the counter. He's the red-faced man who was shouting and scolding the boy down at the dock the day before. As he helps Aunt Märta, he keeps shooting curious glances in Stephie's direction.

36

Something about the look in his eyes makes Stephie very uncomfortable.

When they're about to leave, a young girl walks through the door. It's the same blond girl who made her friends laugh outside Auntie Alma's yard. Her hair is wet and there's a towel flung over her shoulders. She steps confidently behind the counter and fills a bag with toffees. Just helps herself, not asking anyone, and apparently not needing to pay.

The shopkeeper smiles, patting her cheek. The girl pops a toffee in her mouth, chewing and making smacking noises. She stares at Stephie the whole time, until she makes her way to the door and closes it behind her. When Stephie and Aunt Märta get out onto the shop steps, Stephie sees the girl vanish around a bend in the road on her bright blue bicycle.

seven

When Stephie and Aunt Märta return to Auntie Alma's, Nellie is waiting by the gate. Her eyes are bright and she shouts as soon as she sees them:

"Stephie, Stephie, we're going swimming!"

"But we don't have bathing suits."

"Oh, don't we?" Nellie cries triumphantly, swinging a bathing suit out from behind her back. "I do!"

"Where'd you get it?"

"Auntie Alma had it waiting for me," Nellie tells her. "I'm sure Aunt Märta has one for you, too. Auntie Alma says we're just going to eat and go."

"How do you know? You don't understand Swedish!"

"Oh, yes I do. I understand everything Auntie Alma says to me."

Their new "aunts" are standing talking by the fence.

38

When Aunt Märta bikes off, Auntie Alma points to Nellie's bathing suit.

"What did I tell you?" Nellie says delightedly. "You'll get one, too."

Nellie's bathing suit is made of shiny yellow fabric. Stephie hopes hers will be the same, or maybe red.

They eat cheese sandwiches and drink milk at Auntie Alma's kitchen table. The little ones are excited; John spills his milk all over the table. Auntie Alma doesn't get angry. She just wipes it up and pours him a new mug.

Soon Aunt Märta is back, a towel in one hand and something black in the other. She gives them to Stephie. The black thing is a bathing suit. A real old-fashioned lady's bathing suit made of thick wool.

Stephie stares at it. The woolen fabric is so ancient it's going green in spots. Auntie Alma smiles encouragingly. Aunt Märta looks expectant.

"Danke schön," Stephie whispers through stiff lips. Thank you very much.

"Stephie," Nellie whispers, "is that supposed to be a bathing suit? Are you going to wear it?"

"Hush up," Stephie hisses. "One more word and I'll pinch you black and blue."

Nellie goes silent. Auntie Alma has all the other suits and towels in a bag and is waiting by the door. There's no choice for Stephie but to join everyone. She's relieved, at least, to see Aunt Märta head home on her bike.

They walk down a path to the swimming cove. Auntie Alma holds her son by the hand. Nellie and Elsa run loops around the others, racing, pushing one another, laughing.

Stephie lags behind, the awful bathing suit between her thumb and index finger, touching as little of the fabric as possible. Where the path ends there are a few bikes parked, leaned haphazardly against one another. Stephie rolls the bathing suit into her towel.

The narrow strip of sandy beach is full of pebbles. No deck chairs, no beach parasols, no ice cream vendors are in sight. One young mother is on a blanket with three toddlers. No one else is on the beach, but on the cliffs in the distance Stephie sees a group of bigger children, some of whom are in the water below. A head of red hair glistens in the sun.

Auntie Alma spreads a blanket on the sand, sits down on it, and undoes the top two buttons of her blouse. She helps little John into his bathing trunks. Nellie and Elsa undress, pull their suits on, and rush down to the water's edge. They splash and play, chasing each other in the shallow water. Then they lie on their stomachs, pretending to swim.

Stephie sits down on the blanket next to Auntie Alma, who looks inquisitively at her and her bundle. Auntie Alma unrolls the towel and holds up the bathing suit.

"No," says Stephie in German. "I'm not going to swim."

Auntie Alma talks and gesticulates, holding out a hand to Stephie and offering to walk her down to the water. Stephie shakes her head stubbornly, until Auntie Alma gives up. Removing her shoes and stockings, Auntie Alma walks to the water's edge with little John. He puts his feet into the water tentatively, wriggling his toes.

Out on the headland, the older children are jumping off the cliff. Stephie hears their voices clearly, watches them

shoving and laughing, seeing who dares to jump first. The
girls she saw outside Auntie Alma's house are all there,
along with a couple of boys. The blond girl from the shop
has a white bathing suit that ties in the back with a red
band. The redhead's suit is green.

Nellie comes running, shaking herself like a wet puppy.
When she swishes her braids, drops of water splash on
Stephie.

"The water's nice and warm, Stephie," she shouts.
"Aren't you coming in?"

"Nope," Stephie says angrily.

"Why not?"

"None of your business."

"Oh, come on," Nellie insists. "I want to swim together."

"I wouldn't put that sickening suit on if you paid me,"
Stephie replies. "Not on my life."

"Well, if that's how you feel, I guess you can't swim,"
says Nellie reasonably. "I'll be in the water all afternoon,
though," she adds.

She looks pleased with herself, standing there in her yellow suit. Before Stephie can stop herself, she has grabbed a
handful of gravelly sand and tossed it at Nellie. Just at her
legs, but Nellie begins to cry and Auntie Alma comes running. She grabs Stephie by one shoulder and gives her a
shake. Then she comforts Nellie, leading her back to the
water to rinse off.

Stephie stays on the blanket, perspiring in the sunshine.
If she hadn't been mean to Nellie, she might have taken off
her shoes and waded in the shallow water. But now she just
stays where she is, watching Nellie and Elsa collect seashells

along the shore while Auntie Alma plays with John. The blanket is like her own little island.

The kids out on the rocks are getting out of the water. Some of the girls giggle as they take turns holding up towels for each other while they change out of their suits. The boys keep trying to get a peek.

When they pass by Stephie, she looks the other way. She hears a girl say something, but she doesn't move a muscle. If she pretends they aren't there, maybe they'll just disappear. She starts digging in the sand with one hand, staring straight down.

The youngsters go their way, a laughing, chattering crowd. Stephie watches their backs. The blond girl is at the center of the group. When they get to their bikes the redhead turns around, raising a hand in what might be a wave to Stephie.

When Stephie gets home, Aunt Märta points to her rolled-up towel and then to the clothesline that runs from the house to a wooden pole in one corner of the yard. Stephie's first instinct is to show Aunt Märta that neither suit nor towel is wet, but she has second thoughts and just goes over to the line. Seeing a green pump next to the woodshed, she tries it, and it works.

Stephie holds the bathing suit under the pump, wetting it thoroughly. She rolls it back up into the towel and holds it until she sees a damp spot emerge. Then she hangs the suit and towel on the line. Aunt Märta will never know.

eight

Stephie and Nellie's first week on the island is sunny.

Every day, Stephie goes on a long walk from the white frame house at the end of the world to the yellow house with the enclosed veranda.

Every day, Auntie Alma takes the girls along with her own children to the beach.

Every day, Stephie sits on the blanket, fully dressed, watching Nellie and the little ones splashing at the shore, and the older children diving from the cliffs out on the headland.

Auntie Alma probably thinks Stephie doesn't know how to swim and is ashamed to show it. In any case, she doesn't make any further attempts to persuade her to go into the water.

One morning Stephie wakes up and doesn't see the sun

shining in; she's relieved. It's a cloudy, gray day, and windy, too. She puts on a sweater before walking to Auntie Alma's. Aunt Märta points to the suit and towel on the line, shaking her head and saying something. Stephie catches the Swedish words for "swim" and "cold."

"Not swim," Stephie says. "Nellie . . ." That exhausts her Swedish vocabulary.

Aunt Märta nods, ushering Stephie into the room with the wall clock. She points to the three.

"Come home. Three o'clock," she says.

Stephie nods. "Three o'clock."

"Evert," Aunt Märta says. "Uncle Evert's coming home."

Stephie pretends to understand. It's easier that way.

◊   ◊   ◊

In Auntie Alma's kitchen Nellie and the little ones are sitting around the table drawing, and Auntie Alma is mixing something in a bowl. She always keeps busy cooking, baking, washing the dishes, polishing, and dusting. But unlike Aunt Märta, who does the housework gravely and resolutely, Auntie Alma never appears to think anything is any trouble. Ladles, dust cloths, and brooms seem to dance in her hands as if working all on their own. She kneads dough lightly on her baking board, and the dishes seem to fly from the sink into the drainer.

Nellie looks up from her drawing. "We're not going to the beach today," she announces.

"Phew," Stephie replies.

She helps herself to a piece of paper and a pencil and begins to draw a girl's face, with large eyes and curly hair. She spends a long time on the mouth, trying to make a thin, arched Cupid's bow. She has to erase it several times before she's satisfied. The girl looks glum. Pretty and sorrowful. A little like Evi, her best friend back in Vienna.

Elsa admires Stephie's drawing. She's been busy drawing princesses with long blond hair and pink ball gowns. John is too little to do anything other than scribble what looks to Stephie like a jumble of lines and spirals.

Stephie walks around to the other side of the table to look over Nellie's shoulder. She's drawn a man and a woman, both on their knees on the sidewalk. Standing over them is a man in a uniform. He's got a pistol in one hand, and is lashing at the couple. Behind them is a shop window, on which someone has written, in big red letters: JEWS.

Stephie recognizes the scene in Nellie's drawing. She was there, too, one day just after the Germans invaded Vienna, nearly a year and a half ago.

The girls had been on their way home from the playground. Outside the furrier's shop, where their mother bought her fur coats, they saw the furrier and his wife on their knees, scouring the sidewalk with scrub brushes. A man in uniform was guarding them, a pistol in his hand. They were surrounded by a crowd. No one stepped in to help the elderly couple. On the contrary, people were laughing and mocking them. Someone had written JEW in yard-high red letters across their shop window. Stephie took Nellie by the hand and ran home.

"You shouldn't be drawing things like that," she says to Nellie. "Make something pretty instead." She grabs Nellie's drawing and crumples it into a ball.

"What did you do that for?" Nellie protests.

"Draw something nice," Stephie says. "Something for Auntie Alma."

But Nellie doesn't feel like drawing anymore.

"Come with me and I'll show you something," she says to Stephie, pulling her by the hand into the front room. There's an old-fashioned overstuffed couch with a stiff back, a little round table with a crocheted cloth, and armchairs with puffy cushions. There's a little white organ, too. That's what Nellie wants Stephie to see.

"A piano," she says, "there *is* a piano."

"That's not a piano, it's an organ," Stephie corrects her. "You remember, we had one at school."

"Who cares?" Nellie says, sitting down on the organ bench. Her short legs just barely allow her to reach the pedals.

"I'm allowed to play it. Auntie Alma said so."

She starts playing a children's song, while Stephie investigates everything in the room. Against one wall, she sees a glass-paned cupboard filled with knickknacks: a little box decorated with all kinds of seashells, a porcelain basket full of china rosebuds, two statuettes—a shepherd and shepherdess—and many other treasures.

There's even a small china dog. It's brown and white, with a gold-tipped, rather than a black, nose. It has a blue collar and is standing with its head cocked.

"Nellie," Auntie Alma calls from the kitchen. Nellie

stops playing, hops down from the organ bench, and runs out of the room.

Stephie remains mesmerized by the china dog. It's adorable and she longs to hold it. She notices a brass key in the cupboard door. She turns it, opens the door, and carefully removes the dog. The china feels cool in the palm of her hand. She inspects the dog from every angle, stroking it gently.

"Mimi," she whispers. "Your name is Mimi."

"Stephie!" Auntie Alma is standing in the doorway.

Instantly, without thinking, Stephie drops the dog into her dress pocket. She closes the door of the cupboard surreptitiously with her elbow.

Auntie Alma has set out sandwiches and milk on the kitchen table. Stephie eats only a little. She knows she's a guest at Auntie Alma's house, an extra mouth to feed. When Auntie Alma passes the platter toward her again, she says no thanks.

"I'm not . . . hungry," she says slowly, testing her Swedish.

Stephie clasps the china dog in her pocket. She'll put it back as soon as she gets a chance.

After lunch, Auntie Alma sends them out to play. She needs to clean the house, and doesn't want all the children underfoot.

The little china dog in Stephie's pocket upsets her; she feels almost feverish. Holding one hand around it so it won't bump and break, she sits still on the bench in the yard, waiting for Auntie Alma to call them in so she can put it back. That never happens.

Through an open window, Stephie hears the kitchen clock chime. Once, twice, three times. It's three already. She has to leave.

"I need to go home," she calls to Nellie.

Mimi will have to go with her to Aunt Märta's white frame house. Surely there will be a chance to put her back tomorrow morning.

nine

Stephie hurries home, running most of the way. As she opens the door she hears the clock chime once: three-fifteen.

Aunt Märta comes out of the kitchen. She doesn't seem upset. In fact, she almost looks happy.

"Come along, now," she says, leading Stephie back through the kitchen and into the front room.

A man is sitting in the rocking chair. When Stephie enters the room he rises and walks toward her. He has on blue workingman's trousers and a knitted sweater. The hand he extends is large, warm, and calloused. His face is sunburned and lined. The clothes he's wearing smell fishy.

"Uncle Evert," Aunt Märta explains.

"Stephie," says Stephie.

"I wish you a warm welcome to our home," the man says in a soft voice.

"Thank you," Stephie replies in Swedish.

"She understood, Märta! Did you hear that? She understood me!"

"Yes, she's beginning to pick up a few words," Aunt Märta replies. Then she goes into the kitchen to prepare dinner.

Uncle Evert sits back down in the rocking chair. Stephie takes a seat opposite him, and they consider each other. Uncle Evert has bright blue eyes that give Stephie the impression he can see right through her and out into the wide world. Almost as if he has been staring at the ocean for so long it has taken up residence in his eyes.

Eventually Uncle Evert breaks the silence. He speaks slowly, ransacking his memory for German words.

"*Ich . . . Fischer.*" He points to the ocean. "*Farhren weit . . . mit Boot.*"

Stephie nods eagerly. Uncle Evert's German is almost worse than her Swedish, but she understands what he means. That he's a fisherman and has been off on the ocean with his boat.

Tentatively, they converse in a combination of Swedish, German, and sign language. Stephie tells him that her father is a doctor and her mother was an opera singer when she was young, before she had a family. Uncle Evert explains that he started out as a sailor, which was how he learned a little German a long time ago.

"Hamburg," he says. "Bremerhaven, Amsterdam." And Stephie understands that he is telling her the boat he worked on traveled to the big ports in northern Germany and Holland. This is the first time since she arrived on the island that she has been able to talk with someone other than Nellie. She wishes they could go on talking all the way to bedtime.

"Evert," Aunt Märta calls from the kitchen. "Dinner's almost ready."

Uncle Evert gets up. "Wash . . . *waschen* . . . ," he says, pointing to his work clothes. He vanishes up the stairs.

Stephie goes into the kitchen to set the table. Three plates, three glasses, three forks, and three knives, instead of the usual two.

Something hard bumps against her left thigh. The china dog! She's forgotten all about it. What if it breaks! Or what if Aunt Märta notices the bulge in her pocket and asks what it is. She has to hide it in a safe place. As soon as she hears that Uncle Evert has stopped making noise at the washstand and has gone into his bedroom, Stephie extends her hands toward Aunt Märta and imitates his word.

"*Wash* . . ."

Aunt Märta nods approvingly. Stephie rushes up the stairs and into her room. Wrapping Mimi in a handkerchief, she hides the china dog at the very back of the bottom dresser drawer, along with her most treasured possessions. Then she hurries out and washes her hands.

At the table, hands folded, she and Uncle Evert listen to Aunt Märta say grace.

"Come, Lord Jesus, be our guest. Let this food for us be blessed."

"Amen," all three of them conclude.

51

While they eat, Aunt Märta and Uncle Evert talk about his fishing trip and about the news on the island during his absence. Stephie grasps a word here and there. She pokes around at her portion of cod, removing the slimy gray skin and mashing the fish with her potatoes and gravy. The whole thing becomes an unappetizing white mess.

As usual, she rinses down her bites of food with milk, and as usual her milk glass is empty long before her plate is. She rehearses silently several times before trying out her new Swedish phrase, the one she heard little Elsa say just a few hours earlier.

"Would you please pass the milk?"

Aunt Märta's chin drops, and she stops talking mid-sentence.

"Well, I never . . . !" Uncle Evert exclaims. "Just listen to that perfect Swedish!"

"She's a quick learner," Aunt Märta adds, passing Stephie the milk pitcher.

"That's good." Uncle Evert smiles encouragingly from across the table. "It won't be long until you sound just like the rest of us when you speak Swedish. Then you'll be able to go to school."

Stephie doesn't really catch his meaning. But she does recognize the Swedish word for school.

"Please," she says. "School."

She thinks about her old school in Vienna. Her real school, where she was the top student in her class and always got gold stars for her assignments. Where her teacher liked her—or at least Stephie believed so, until one day in March last year.

The day after the German army invaded Vienna, her teacher came to school with a swastika pinned to her pretty blazer.

"*Heil Hitler!*" she began the day by saying to the class. No more "Good morning, children."

"*Heil Hitler!*" some of the students responded, raising an arm in the prescribed salute. Others just stared, unsure as to what the teacher expected of them.

They soon learned. From that day on, she told them, they were all expected to start the day with "*Heil Hitler!*" All but the Jewish children, that is, who were not allowed to perform the Hitler salute. For that reason, the teacher told them, they must sit apart, in the back row of desks, so she could be sure that all the German children, and none of the Jewish ones, were doing the salute correctly.

An incredulous mumble rose from the room. What was she saying? Could she possibly mean it?

"Well . . . ?" their teacher said, a stern expression on her face. "Did you hear me?"

The class monitor, Irene, got up, taking her books from her desk, and moved from the front row to an empty desk in the far corner at the back of the room. A few others followed. Some of the children who had always sat in the back row left their desks and moved forward to the ones now free. Stephie and Evi didn't budge from their seats, which were directly in front of the teacher's lectern.

"You, too, Stephie!" her teacher said sharply. "And Evi."

"But I'm not Jewish," Evi cried. "My mother's Catholic."

"That makes no difference," the teacher said coldly. "Go sit at the back."

Evi got up from behind her desk and rushed out of the room, slamming the door behind her. There was total silence.

"Come, now," the teacher said to Stephie. "Do as you're told."

Stephie gathered up her books and moved to an empty desk at the back. The teacher then picked up a piece of chalk and, without another word, started writing arithmetic problems on the blackboard.

"What are you sitting there dreaming about?" Uncle Evert asks kindly.

"Don't play with your food," Aunt Märta scolds at the same time.

Stephie snaps back to the present. Looking down at her plate, she's surprised to see that she has been drawing something in her mashed potatoes with her fork. A star. Like the gold stars in her assignment books. Like the star of David that stands for "Jewish." Quickly she gives her mashed-up food a stir and begins to eat again.

ten

Uncle Evert stays home for two days. When he leaves again Stephie goes along to the harbor to wave goodbye. The fishing boat has a crew of six. The youngest member, Per-Erik, isn't much older than Stephie, and when the two are introduced, Per-Erik shyly looks away. Auntie Alma's husband, Sigurd, is also a member of the crew.

Uncle Evert has told Stephie that the boat is named the *Diana.* Stephie likes that name, but all it says on the bow of the boat is GG 143, to show that it is vessel 143 of the Göteborg fishing fleet.

After Uncle Evert leaves, things return to normal. Stephie has breakfast with Aunt Märta every morning, after which she puts things away and washes the dishes. Then she spends the rest of the day with Nellie, until it's time to go home for dinner. After dinner she washes the dishes again, and helps Aunt Märta with other chores. In the evenings she either sits in her room or in the window nook writing letters or entries in her diary.

Inside the back cover of her diary she makes a short line for every day she's been on the island. There are 182 days in six months. Every evening she counts the lines. *Thirty-four, thirty-five, thirty-six . . .*

In her letters to her parents, she tells them everything is fine. She does the same when she writes to Evi, except that she conjures a particularly lovely picture of life on the island. She hopes that if she makes Sweden sound tempting enough, Evi will want to come, too. But she knows that since Evi's mother is Catholic, Evi may not have to leave Austria at all.

When Stephie isn't writing, she's reading. Soon she's read every single book she brought from home. The only book in Aunt Märta's white frame house is the Bible on the table in the front room.

"When are we going home, Stephie?" Nellie asks. "Can we leave soon?"

"We're not going home," Stephie explains patiently, "and you know it. We're going to America. As soon as Mamma and Papa get their entry visas, we'll meet them in Amsterdam."

"When will that be?" Nellie asks for the hundredth time.

"I don't know. Soon."

They're huddled close together on a big rock at the beach. The water glistens a beautiful shade of blue in the sun, but the wind is chilly and no one swims anymore. It's September and all the other children have started school.

Stephie and Nellie have the beach to themselves now; it's the place where they can be alone with their homesickness.

"Tell me about America," Nellie begs.

"In America," Stephie tells her, "things aren't at all like here. They have big cities with tall buildings and streets full of cars."

"Like in Vienna?"

"The buildings are much taller. Everything in America is huge. We'll live in a house with lots and lots of rooms and a big garden. A real garden with tall trees, lindens and chestnuts. Almost a park. Not at all like here."

"Will we have a dog there?" Nellie asks.

Stephie remembers Mimi, the china dog wrapped in a handkerchief in the bottom of her dresser drawer. Auntie Alma must have noticed the dog is missing. With every passing day it becomes increasingly difficult to put Mimi back.

"Yes, of course we will," Stephie answers simply.

"And a piano," Nellie adds. "We *will* have a piano in America, won't we?"

When they have had enough of sitting and talking they wander the narrow streets of the village. Not that there's much to see. Houses and yards, mounds of rock. The post office, the shop, the schoolhouse. A little chapel on a rise hovers above the other buildings. At the edge of the village, not far from Auntie Alma's, is a big red building people call the Pentecostal Church, though it doesn't look much like a church at all. And near the harbor there's another, the Mission Covenant Church.

Down at the harbor there's always something happening.

Boats coming and going. Fishermen cleaning out their nets and repairing their boats. Above each boathouse is a name. Stephie reads them: JUNO, INEZ, SWEDEN, MATILDA, NORTH SEA . . . Now she knows that the hanging triangular shapes she once thought were bats are splayed fish drying on long wooden racks.

There are always some older men on the benches of the boathouses, talking and smoking their pipes. One of them offers the girls a piece of candy from his bag whenever they pass by. These are hard candies, dark red, sweet and pungent.

One day a freighter has pulled in. Two of the crew members are working on deck.

"I'll bet they're headed for Hamburg," Stephie says. "Or Amsterdam."

"Amsterdam!" Nellie exclaims. "Isn't that where we'll be going, too?"

"Right."

Nellie walks over to the edge of the dock. "Can we come along?" she asks one of the sailors. "We want to get to Amsterdam."

The man responds in Swedish, then goes back to what he was doing.

"I don't think he understood what I meant," Nellie says to Stephie. "Why don't you try?"

Stephie knows their parents are still in Vienna. They can't leave until they have their entry visas for America. Still, she, too, feels they'd be closer to each other if she and Nellie were in Amsterdam.

"Oh, please," Stephie appeals to the sailor. "Won't you take us along? We're going to Amsterdam."

The sailor looks down at her, shaking his head with a smile.

Boat tickets cost money. That must be why he won't take the girls.

Stephie turns her dress pockets inside out to show they don't have any money.

"Gypsy kids," one man says to the other. "How do you think they ended up here?"

He forages in his own pocket, then throws something to Stephie. She catches it in her hand: it's a small, shiny coin.

The crew members are done with their work. One of them starts untying the mooring ropes.

"Please!" Stephie shouts. "Please don't leave without us!"

The boat pulls away from the dock. Slowly it glides out toward the harbor entrance. Stephie begins to run along the dock and out onto the breakwater. Nellie is close on her heels.

"Take us with you! Take us with you!" the two of them cry.

The freighter rounds the breakwater and is on the open sea. The men wave to the girls.

"We're shipwrecked," says Stephie. "Alone on a desert island. A ship passed, but it didn't see our smoke signals. We'll have to wait for the next one."

"Will anybody save us?" Nellie asks.

"Oh, yes," says Stephie. "We'll be rescued next time around."

They stand, watching from the breakwater, until the freighter disappears against the horizon. Then, slowly, they make their way toward the village.

On the dock is a big, awkward-looking boy in clothes that are too small for him. Stephie recognizes him. He spends almost every afternoon down at the harbor, helping clean the nets and bail out the dinghies. When the steamboat from town comes in, he brings deliveries ashore for the shopkeeper.

"Want a boat ride?" he asks them. "I've got a boat, too, you know."

He looks at Stephie expectantly. His mouth gapes, his face is pimply.

"No," Stephie says, pulling Nellie along. She picks up speed to pass him by.

"Are you sad, Stephie?" Nellie asks her. "Because the sailors wouldn't take us?"

Stephie doesn't answer.

"I'm not upset," Nellie tells her. "I'd rather go home."

"We're not ever going to be able to go home," Stephie sputters. "Don't you see?"

"You're mean to me," Nellie cries. "I'm going to tell Mamma how mean you're being."

She starts to run up the street. Stephie runs after her, grabbing her by one braid.

"Ow," Nellie whines, aiming a kick at Stephie's leg.

Stephie holds on to Nellie tightly, looking her straight in the eye.

"You're not going to write a single word about this to Mamma, do you hear? Especially not about wanting to go

home. You mustn't write anything that will make her unhappy. Understand?"

Nellie stares angrily down at her feet and nods.

"Promise?"

Nellie nods again. Stephie lets her go, and Nellie takes a
few steps back to get beyond her sister's reach.

"But I'm going to tell Auntie Alma," she shouts over her
shoulder as she turns and runs down the street.

eleven

There's a war on in Europe now. Papa has written and described what happened: Germany invaded Poland, then England and France declared war on Germany. Because Austria is part of the German empire, this means that Stephie's country is also at war.

We don't really know what this will mean for us yet, her father wrote. *It may be more difficult to get out of the country, or just the opposite: perhaps America and other nations that are not involved in the war will now be more willing to take in refugees. Time will tell.*

During her rambles around the island, Stephie spends a lot of time thinking about all the things her father's letter didn't say. Will Papa have to join the army? Or be sent back to the labor camp? Will passenger boats be crossing the

Atlantic during the war? Might the war spread all the way to Sweden?

One day Stephie invents a new game.

"Now we're in Vienna," she tells Nellie.

Nellie looks around, bewildered. "We are?"

"Don't you see?" Stephie insists. "We're walking down Kärntnerstrasse; we're on the wide sidewalk there. The street is lined with fancy shops on both sides." She points to the bedrock rising on either side of the path.

"The shop windows are bright," she continues, "and full of beautiful things. Clothes, shoes, fur coats, perfume. Do you see?"

Nellie nods eagerly.

"Close your eyes," Stephie tells her. "Listen carefully. Can you hear the clattering of the tramway, and the passing cars?"

She shuts her own eyes, too, listening. When you aren't looking you can easily imagine that the breaking waves sound like traffic noises.

"Here comes a tram," Nellie shouts. "And another."

"Right," Stephie agrees. "Now we're passing the opera house. Remember when we got to go see *The Magic Flute*? You were so little you fell asleep in the middle of the second act. Now we're turning the corner up toward Heldenplatz. Look, there's the statue of the horseman. And an old lady feeding the pigeons."

"I'd rather go to the park," Nellie interrupts her. "To the playground. It's a lot more fun there."

"But we're going in the other direction today," Stephie

63

insists. "Tomorrow you get to decide. Come on, let's cut across Heldenplatz."

"Where are we headed?" Nellie asks.

"To the Freyung to see what's for sale at the market."

"That's a long way," Nellie protests. "I want to go home now."

"No, it's not so far. Close your eyes and hold my hand. We'll be there soon."

Stephie shuts her eyes again, almost feeling as if she really were on the narrow streets of the old town. She has to think about every step so as not to stumble on the rough path. Pretending the bumps are cobblestones rather than rocks and roots, she goes on.

The sound of footsteps disturbs their fantasy game. Stephie's eyes snap open.

On the path in front of them is the girl with the red hair. She smiles and tosses her hair; it blows in the wind.

"Hello!" she says. "My name's Vera. What are yours?"

"Stephie."

Nellie stands silently, eyes lowered. Stephie gives her a nudge.

"Nellie," she says softly, not looking at Vera.

"Come on," says Vera, motioning for them to follow her. They scale a low stone wall and cross a slope with dry grass and heather before arriving at a crevice in the bedrock. There's a tangle of thorny bushes there. Big, black berries shine out among the leaves. Vera picks a few and extends them in the palm of her hand. Stephie hesitates. Is this a nasty joke? Will the berries be bitter, so they'll have to spit them out? Will Vera laugh at them?

"Stephie, are they poison?" Nellie whispers from behind her.

Stephie takes a berry and puts it in her mouth. It's sweet and tasty. She takes another.

"So they're not poison?" Nellie asks, reaching out. Vera gives her a few berries. Nellie puts them all in her mouth at once. "Yum," she declares. There's deep purple juice on her lips.

"Blackberries," Vera explains. "Haven't you ever tasted them before? Black berries, not black bears!"

She begins imitating a bear: crawling on all fours and growling loudly. When Vera rears up on her back legs, Nellie is doubled over with laughter. But suddenly Nellie becomes serious.

"Stephie, are there any bears here? For real?"

"No," Stephie reassures her. "Bears live in big forests. There are hardly even any trees on this island."

Nellie peeks suspiciously into the deep crevice in the bedrock. "Are you sure?"

"Absolutely," Stephie replies. "I promise."

But as her eyes follow Nellie's into the rock crevice, she, too, begins to wonder what other wild, dangerous animals could be hiding in there.

They all pick berries, eating them right off the bushes, and soon their fingers are all purple. Vera laughs and prattles. Stephie answers, using the few words of Swedish she knows.

Stephie's skirt gets caught on a thorny branch. She tries to disentangle it, but the thorns grip like claws and refuse to let go. Stephie pulls harder. The cloth rips with a loud sound.

She stares down at her skirt; a gaping hole stares back. Next to it is a berry stain from her hands. What will Aunt Märta say?

Vera looks frightened. Only Nellie continues picking and eating the berries as if she didn't have a care in the world.

"Have to go home," Stephie tells Vera.

Vera nods understandingly. "Fix it," she says, making sewing motions.

The three girls walk part of the way together. Then Vera turns off, up a path so narrow it's almost invisible. With a wave and a smile she's gone.

Stephie decides to go straight home. If she's lucky Aunt Märta will be out, and even if she's at home, Stephie ought to be able to sneak up the stairs and change her dress. She has another very similar one, and Aunt Märta probably won't recall which one Stephie wore that morning. She'll take the torn one in her knapsack to Auntie Alma's tomorrow morning. Surely Auntie Alma will be able to show her how to mend the rip and remove the stain. Aunt Märta will never need to know.

Stephie and Nellie part when they get to the yellow house. Continuing on, Stephie reaches the crest of the hill and looks to see if she can spot Aunt Märta's bicycle. She's in luck. The bike isn't leaning against the house. She hurries down the slope and runs the rest of the way. She pulls open the door, then lets it slam behind her. She hears footsteps coming down, but she's already halfway up the stairs. Too late to escape.

Aunt Märta's eyes are drawn like magnets to Stephie's torn, stained skirt.

"I'm sorry," Stephie stammers.

"Go straight to your room," Aunt Märta instructs her. "Take off that dress and have a wash. You will stay in your room for the rest of the day."

Stephie does as she's told. As usual, she folds her dress over the back of the chair and goes out to the washstand. She doesn't dare to put a clean one on afterward, simply pulls on her nightgown over her undergarments, although it's still broad daylight.

Aunt Märta comes into the room, gathers up the dress, and goes out again without a word. The door bangs shut behind her.

Stephie opens her bottom dresser drawer. Removing the china dog from its handkerchief, she stands it next to her photographs. Then she takes out her jewelry box and opens the lid. Soft music plays and a ballerina begins to turn on her pointed leg. The jewelry box was a present from her mother on Stephie's tenth birthday. When the music stops, she shuts the lid and opens it again. The ballerina turns and dances once more.

"Mamma," she whispers to the picture. "Mamma, I want to come home."

She hears noise from the kitchen. After a while the smell of food wafts up, but Aunt Märta doesn't call her. Then there's more noise, followed by silence.

Stephie hasn't eaten anything but blackberries since breakfast. Even fish would taste good right now.

67

Not until several hours later does Aunt Märta bring her up a glass of milk and some bread and butter. She puts the plate down by the window. As she is leaving, she turns around.

"Vera Hedberg. What kind of company is that to keep?" Aunt Märta says. "Sloppy and trashy, just like her mother."

She closes the door behind her so fast Stephie doesn't have time to ask what she means. What's wrong with Vera and her mother?

When Stephie sits down by the window to eat, she notices Aunt Märta's bicycle leaning up against the woodshed. The chain has come off.

twelve

On a Sunday evening toward the end of September, Aunt Märta tells Stephie to put her coat on. They're going to a "revival meeting," she explains. Stephie doesn't have the slightest idea what that means, but she pulls on her coat obediently and goes along. They walk into the village and toward the rectangular wooden house called the Pentecostal Church.

A big crowd is gathered outside. Some people have started to go in, others stand chatting in groups. Auntie Alma is there, too, with Nellie and the little ones.

"What kind of place is this?" Nellie asks Stephie in a whisper.

"I'm not sure," Stephie whispers back. "Some kind of church, though."

Inside, there is one big room with rows of wooden

benches. In some ways it resembles the churches in Vienna. But in Vienna churches are old stone buildings with stained glass windows, icons, and the scent of hundreds of lit candles. Stephie's been in churches like that with Evi and her mother.

Here, there is nothing but a great big, bare room with a raised lectern, like in a classroom. No candles cast their flickering light over mysterious aisles and stone columns. No images of saints gaze solemnly down. There's only the glare from the electric light fixture on the ceiling. The wooden floor smells newly scrubbed.

The benches are filling up. Stephie sits between Aunt Märta and Nellie. Auntie Alma has John on her lap on the other side of Nellie, and then comes Elsa.

When everyone is seated, the revival meeting begins.

A tall, thin man stands at the lectern speaking in a monotonous voice. He holds his big hands in front of him, gesturing emphatically to stress his point. Stephie doesn't understand everything he's saying, but it's about God and Jesus and sinners who ought to repent.

"Come home to Jesus," the man says. "He will embrace you, whoever you may be."

Sometimes he uses expressions that make Stephie sit up with a jolt. He speaks of "flaming arrows aimed at our hearts" and "the blood of the lamb." Unusual, poetic words.

In the row behind them is a woman who can't seem to stop mumbling to herself.

"Oh, sweet Jesus," she says over and over again. Stephie turns around to look at her, but instantly feels Aunt Märta's elbow nudge her in the side. Aunt Märta sits ramrod straight, her hands clasped tightly in her lap and her mouth firmly shut.

The bench is hard. On Stephie's other side, Nellie is squirming.

Suddenly a woman at the very front gets up and begins to speak. She rambles on, babbling the same words over and over again. Stephie strains to listen but understands not a single word. It doesn't sound like Swedish, or like any other language Stephie has ever heard.

Stephie and Nellie glance at each other. Stephie's afraid she may burst out laughing, though she can tell from Aunt Märta's stern profile that she mustn't.

Now the thin man starts babbling, too. And he gesticulates as he speaks.

During the High Holy Days every autumn Stephie and Nellie would go to the synagogue with their parents. At temple you didn't have to sit still the whole time. People came and went, stood outside the sanctuary chatting, saying hello to friends and wishing one another a happy holiday. The children would run around in the yard when they needed a break, then go back in and sit with their parents again. Up in the balcony, where Stephie and Nellie sat with Mamma looking down at Papa and the other men, ladies who smelled of perfume would pass around bags of candy.

On the tenth day, the Day of Atonement, however, everyone was solemn and silent. Last fall lots of people wept when the rabbi read the prayer for the dead. Only a few weeks later the synagogue was gone—burned down on a terrible night in November. The same night that—

She isn't going to think about it. With effort, Stephie

71

focuses her attention on the present. The thin man is looking out over the congregation.

"Jesus Christ," he says. "Jesus Christ is the answer to all your questions."

All your questions! Could Jesus explain why she had to be sent to a foreign country? Could he tell her and Nellie when they will see Mamma and Papa again?

Now the thin man steps aside. A group of young people come up to the lectern. Something about their red cheeks and bright eyes makes them look alike. They don't seem to have a single question in the world.

They begin to sing, their voices clear. A young woman, her braids pinned up on top of her head, accompanies the choir on a guitar. This is the first music Stephie has heard since her arrival. The songs flow through her, filling her, warming her. She closes her eyes and feels pleasure course through her body. The music is so lovely, she can't stop herself from crying.

Nellie touches her arm gently. Stephie seizes Nellie's hand and holds it tight. Nellie begins to cry, too. They weep throughout the singing, until the final tones fade away. Aunt Märta gets up and urges the sisters ahead of her down the aisle.

At the altar, Aunt Märta falls to her knees. Stephie and Nellie follow suit, kneeling on either side of her. The thin man puts one of his large hands on Stephie's head, the other on Nellie's, and prays in a loud voice.

Stephie can feel everyone in the room staring at them. Has she misbehaved? Should she ask forgiveness? The floor is hard, and a splinter is piercing her stocking and poking her knee.

Take me away from here, she prays silently. She doesn't know to whom this prayer is addressed. God? Jesus? Papa? Mamma?

"Amen," says the thin man.

"Amen," the congregation responds in unison.

Aunt Märta gets up. Stephie totters to her feet, too. It's over.

Now everyone is singing. They go back to their seats. Auntie Alma gives Nellie a hug. Then she reaches over and pats Stephie on the cheek.

After the revival meeting they go back to Auntie Alma's.

"My, my," says Aunt Märta. "I never imagined the girls would embrace Jesus so quickly. Who would have thought it?"

"They're only girls," Auntie Alma replies. "There's not a drop of evil in them. They can't be blamed for being born outside the true faith."

"So something good has come of it," Aunt Märta puffs. "Their souls have found a home."

"What did you do it for, Stephie?" Nellie asks. "What made you cry?"

"The music," Stephie answers. "It was so beautiful. And what made you cry?"

"*Your* tears," Nellie replies.

Auntie Alma turns to the girls. "How gratified you must be," she says, "to have found Jesus and been redeemed. I'm very happy for you!"

Found Jesus? Been redeemed? Slowly Stephie begins to understand that Aunt Märta and Auntie Alma imagine it was Jesus who made her weep.

"Well," she begins hesitantly, "the music was so beautiful . . ."

But Auntie Alma's not listening. She's still talking to Aunt Märta, the two of them discussing the thin pastor.

"He has the gift," Aunt Märta says. "Yes, he truly has the gift."

Stephie stays quiet.

A few weeks later she and Nellie are baptized. They don't protest. And now that they're members of the Pentecostal Church, they go to Sunday school every week.

Stephie has a feeling she ought to be different now that she's been redeemed. Maybe nicer, more obedient. Surely that's what Aunt Märta expects. But Stephie feels exactly the same as before. Sometimes she sits looking at the picture of Jesus above her dresser, trying to feel the love for him about which they speak at Sunday school, but she feels nothing in particular.

"Forgive me, Jesus," she mumbles softly. "Forgive me if I'm not really and truly redeemed."

Stephie doesn't write to her mother and father about being redeemed or baptized. She doesn't know how she could ever explain it. It might upset them. She wonders if a person can get un-redeemed later. Otherwise she'll have to keep it secret forever, after the family is reunited.

At least Sunday school offers a break from their every-day routines. The Sunday school teacher is the girl who played the guitar. They often sing. A younger girl named

Britta gives Stephie a bookmark angel with dark hair and a pink dress. She has another one, too, a blond one in a blue dress, but she doesn't want to give that one away.

Britta and Stephie are the same age, but Britta's shorter. She has dull, straggly brown hair. Sometimes she walks Stephie partway home after Sunday school.

Vera doesn't attend Sunday school. Stephie sees her now and then, but she's always with the same group of girls, including the blonde whose father is the shopkeeper, plus another who's much bigger and heavier.

The only one who ever says hello when Stephie sees them is Vera. The others just stare. Once, the blonde shouts something after her, but Stephie doesn't catch the words.

thirteen

The schoolhouse for the older children is right in the middle of the village—a yellow, two-story wooden building with a clock over the entrance. On the other side of the street is a second building where the very youngest children's classrooms are; it's not much larger than a regular house.

Sometimes Stephie and Nellie pass the school buildings on their ramblings. If it's recess and the children are out in the schoolyard the sisters walk slowly, peeking at the noisy boys and girls at play.

"When will *we* start school?" Nellie asks.

"As soon as our Swedish is good enough," Stephie answers.

"I'm good at Swedish," Nellie says with pride. "Auntie Alma says I'm a real chatterbox."

It's true that Nellie already speaks very good Swedish, better than Stephie. That's because she can talk to both Auntie Alma and Elsa whenever she pleases. Aunt Märta isn't exactly generous with words, and Uncle Evert is seldom home.

"We'll be fluent enough to start school soon," Stephie says. She gazes longingly over the fence, glimpsing a head of red hair that has to be Vera's. If only Stephie were allowed to go to school, she'd see Vera every day and surely they'd become friends.

At dinner she tries extra hard to pronounce the Swedish words correctly. Hasn't Aunt Märta noticed how much Swedish she has learned? As if she has been reading Stephie's thoughts, Aunt Märta speaks up before she leaves the table.

"I was talking with Auntie Alma this afternoon. We think the time has come for you and Nellie to start school. You can't just wander around all day long. I'm going to speak with the head teacher tomorrow, and I hope you'll be able to start on Monday."

The next morning Aunt Märta bikes over to the school. In the afternoon she tells Stephie she'll be entering sixth grade.

"But I've already completed sixth grade," Stephie protests. "Last year in Vienna."

"You're twelve, aren't you?" Aunt Märta snaps. "So you will be in sixth grade with the other children your age. Where would you go if you weren't? To the grammar school in Göteborg?"

After some time Stephie realizes that Swedish children start school at age seven, not at six as she did back home. So the children her age are in sixth grade, the final year of compulsory school.

Thinking about it, she sees it's probably just as well to repeat sixth grade. She's already missed nearly two months of the fall semester.

Besides, last year in Vienna she didn't really learn very much. First her family had to move to the cramped room, and Stephie had to walk twice as far to school as before. In the crowded quarters, and with the noise of the other tenants, it wasn't easy to concentrate on homework, either. Later in the year she had to change schools, when the Jewish children were no longer allowed to attend regular school.

The classrooms in the Jewish school were overcrowded, the teachers pale from exhaustion and worry. There were no gold stars for their exercise books.

◊   ◊   ◊

The next day Aunt Märta goes to see someone and returns with a pile of schoolbooks. There's a math book, a history book, a science book, an atlas, and a songbook. All are dirty and dog-eared, with the name Per-Erik penned in round, childish letters on the front page of each.

The books belonged to the same Per-Erik who is the youngest member of Uncle Evert's fishing crew. He finished school two years ago. Now Stephie will have to use his old books. Aunt Märta even has a math exercise book with her, less than half full. Stephie stares at the books, blinking back her tears.

"Couldn't I have a new exercise book of my own?" she asks softly.

"Hardly any of this one's been used," Aunt Märta tells her. "Finish it first, then you can have a new one."

Stephie leafs through the roughly treated books. The spine of the science book is ragged. When she opens the book there is no resistance; it opens out like a broken fan. Some of the pages are loose. She remembers the feeling of opening a brand-new book: the way the spine won't give when you try to open it wide, the smell of new paper.

"Don't look so downhearted," Aunt Märta scolds. "I don't have money to waste on new books for your last year of school. Besides, you may not even be here for the entire school year. Old ones will do."

They'll do for me, Stephie finds herself thinking. *Old, worn-out books will do for a foreign child. Old, worn-out books, not to mention an ugly, old lady's bathing suit that will do for a refugee child who has to live off the charity of others. If Aunt Märta had a child of her own, that child would never be getting hand-me-down books.*

"Here," says Aunt Märta, holding out a roll of brown wrapping paper. "Once you've covered them they'll look much nicer."

Auntie Alma goes all the way to Göteborg to buy schoolbooks for Nellie. Aunt Märta sends some money along to buy the things Stephie still needs: two more exercise books, a few pencils, an eraser, and a New Testament.

"You'll have the Testament for the rest of your life," Aunt Märta tells her. "Schoolbooks are a different matter."

Nellie's books also get covered in brown paper.

"I promise to take very good care of them," Nellie says.

When Auntie Alma's back is turned, Stephie sticks out her tongue. "Butter her up all you can," she teases.

"You're just jealous," Nellie tells her. "If you were a little nicer, you might get new books, too, you know."

Almost immediately, Nellie regrets her words and extends her math exercise book to Stephie.

"You can have this one if you want," she says.

"What would you do your math homework in, then?" Stephie asks.

"Math's so boring," Nellie answers, making a face.

On Saturday Uncle Evert comes home. He's obviously been told that Stephie's going to start school, because he has brought her a present wrapped in paper from a shop in Göteborg.

The parcel contains a wooden pencil case. The sliding top fits perfectly in its grooves. Along one side of the top are measurement markings. If you slide the top all the way off, you can use it as a ruler. The box has two long, narrow compartments for pens, and a special little space for an eraser.

"Oh, thank you!" Stephie exclaims. "Thank you so much, Uncle Evert."

"You're spoiling the girl," mutters Aunt Märta.

Uncle Evert ignores the comment. "I think you're going to do well in school," he tells Stephie. "You're so alert and interested."

On Sunday evening Stephie packs her things for school, putting all her pencils and her fountain pen into the pencil box, along with her new eraser. The knapsack is heavy.

"It really is a shame you can't ride a bicycle," Aunt

Märta says. "I'd let you use mine and you could do the shopping on your way home. It would save me a trip to the village, since you'll be there anyway."

Everyone on the island rides a bike, or at least all the adults and all the children Stephie's age do. The little ones ride on the carrier or sit on the handlebars. The big kids ride in crowds, jabbering as loudly as the flocks of seagulls that come in from the ocean to gobble morsels on land.

Stephie is the only one who can't ride a bike. And she's positive she'll never learn.

fourteen

On her first school day, Stephie heads off early. It's a cold morning, so she buttons her blue coat all the way up.

Nellie's waiting for her by the gate at Auntie Alma's. Her hair is in braids, with big pink ribbons tied at the ends. Auntie Alma comes out and stands on the steps to wave them off.

The elementary school classrooms are in a white building opposite the big schoolhouse. Nellie's teacher comes out to greet her. She's young and pretty, with blond braids fastened around her head.

Stephie heads across the street and stands outside the fence of the other schoolyard. She watches as lots of children run around, shouting and laughing. The clock over the door is at ten minutes to eight. Ten minutes to go. As she walks through the gate, she scours the yard for Vera, then for Britta from Sunday school, but there's no one she knows.

The time passes slowly. Stephie wishes she could make herself invisible. Although no one seems to notice her, she feels as if everyone is staring. She shouldn't have worn her coat and hat. The other girls just have sweaters over their dresses and are bareheaded, even though it's October. The boys are in shorts and knee socks, which slip down when they run and climb.

The school bell rings. At last, Britta comes running with a jump rope in her hands.

"Come on," she says to Stephie. "You're in my class."

The sixth-grade room is upstairs. The children form two lines, girls to the left of the door, boys to the right.

Vera smiles at Stephie, the special kind of smile you smile at someone with whom you share a secret. Stephie tries to stand next to her in line, but the blond girl shoves her roughly.

"That's my place," she says.

Stephie goes to the back to the line. Britta is right in front of her.

"Pay no attention to Sylvia," Britta whispers, turning around. "She thinks she's in charge."

The bell rings a second time and the classroom door opens. The teacher stands in the doorway, greeting each pupil as they go in, first the girls, and then the boys. Each child remains standing behind his or her desk, except for Stephie, who waits by the door.

The teacher is tall and thin and wears her hair in a bun just like Aunt Märta's.

"Good morning, children," she says to the class.

"Good morning, Miss Bergström," thirty high and low voices reply.

"You may take your seats."

There is slamming and banging as the children settle in.

"We have a new pupil in our class today," Miss Bergström says. "Come to the front, Stephanie."

Stephie walks toward the teacher's desk.

"Stephanie has been on a long journey to get here," Miss Bergström tells the class. "All the way from Vienna. What country is Vienna in? Sylvia?"

"Austria," Sylvia answers.

Miss Bergström pulls on a string and down comes a map in front of the blackboard. A map of Europe.

"Stephanie, would you show us the country you come from?"

Stephie walks over to the map. But she cannot find the familiar outline of Austria. Instead, she just sees Germany, round as a balloon.

"It ought to be here," she says in bewilderment, pointing to the lower part of the balloon.

Miss Bergström studies the map a moment. "Austria has become part of the German Reich," she says with composure. She points. "This is Vienna, the musical capital of the world. And here is the highest mountain chain in Europe. What is it called? Vera?"

"The Himalayas," Vera replies.

The whole class laughs.

Miss Bergström sighs, then asks Britta if she knows the right answer.

"The Alps."

"Stephanie, have you been to the Alps?"

Stephie shakes her head.

"The Alpine landscape," Miss Bergström tells them, "is very fertile and—"

There is a knock at the door.

"Come in," Miss Bergström says in an annoyed tone.

An awkward figure enters the room. It's the boy from down at the dock, the one who offered Stephie and Nellie a ride in his boat.

He has to be at least fourteen. What's he doing here, in the sixth grade?

"Excuse me for being late," the boy mumbles.

Miss Bergström sighs. "Just sit down, Svante."

Svante walks sluggishly, taking a seat at the back of the room. He's so big he just barely fits behind the desk.

Miss Bergström brings the geography lesson to an end.

"Stephanie is a foreigner among us," she says. "Because of this terrible war she has had to leave her home and family."

Stephie gazes out over the fair-haired boys and girls. She meets their gazes, some curious, others sympathetic. Thirty pairs of blue, gray, or green eyes meet her brown ones.

"I hope you will be very kind to Stephanie," Miss Bergström continues. "And that you can overlook the fact that she doesn't talk the way you do. That is because she isn't Swedish, wasn't born here like all of you."

Not-like-you-not-like-you echoes in Stephanie's head. It reminds her of the chug-chugging of the train on the tracks. She feels weak-kneed and dizzy.

"May I sit down now?" she asks.

Miss Bergström nods.

Britta raises her hand. "Could she sit next to me? I know her."

"So do I," says Svante.

Sylvia laughs, whispering something to the heavyset girl at the desk next to hers.

They have math for the first hour. The problems are easy, simple division Stephie learned in fifth grade. She waves her hand eagerly and finally gets a chance to solve one problem at the blackboard.

"Quite right," Miss Bergström tells Stephie when she is done. "Very good."

"Verrrrry good," Sylvia imitates in a whisper. Miss Bergström pretends she hasn't heard.

When recess comes, Stephie hopes Vera will find her, but she doesn't. Vera spends recess in a corner of the schoolyard, among a crowd of girls that includes Sylvia. Sometimes Stephie senses them looking at her. She wonders what they're saying.

Britta, though, seeks her out and asks if she wants to jump rope. Stephie does just fine until she notices Svante staring. Then she gets nervous and misses a step. So she has to turn the rope.

While Britta is jumping, someone comes up behind Stephie. She turns her head and sees Sylvia's whole crowd, with Sylvia in the lead.

"Say something in German," Sylvia commands.

Stephie shakes her head and keeps turning the rope.

"Say something!" Sylvia repeats. "You can talk, can't you?"

"Sure."

"So say something, then," Sylvia nags. "We want to hear how it sounds."

"Say something," one of her friends urges. It's Barbro, the girl who's always with Sylvia.

The group encircles Stephie. Vera stays in the background, pulling up a sock and rummaging through her dress pocket.

"How about a yodel?" Sylvia asks. "You're from the Alps, after all."

Britta misses a step now. She walks over to Stephie's end and takes the rope from her hand.

"Your turn," she says.

"Stop showing off," Sylvia says to Stephie. "Don't think you can butter Miss Bergström up, either. Little Princess from Vienna. Who asked you to come here, anyway?"

Stephie pretends she doesn't understand. She doesn't care what Sylvia thinks.

She runs in under the turning jump rope, counting silently to herself. *One . . . and . . . two . . . and . . . one . . . and . . . two . . . and—*

There's a sudden tug and the rope is pulled tight. Stephie falls down, scraping the palms of her hands on the hard gravel. Sylvia smiles mockingly as she drops the rope and walks off with her entourage.

fifteen

When November arrives, the island is even grayer than it was over the summer. Only the juniper bushes are still green. It's dark when Stephie leaves for school in the morning, and it's dark by the time she returns in the afternoon. She has a long walk. The wind blowing in off the ocean bites right through her coat; her knees go blue with the cold.

Still, she's pleased to be going to school. How would she have made the days pass otherwise? The afternoons and evenings with Aunt Märta are long enough. They never just sit chatting as Stephie and Mamma would.

The minute Stephie walked in after school, she and her mother used to sit down, Mamma with a cup of coffee and Stephie with hot chocolate. Stephie would tell her mother what she had done that day, and what she had seen on her way home. Mamma might tell her a story about her own childhood or about when she performed at the opera. They would talk about the books they were reading, or about the trips they planned to go on together when Stephie was older.

Writing to someone is not the same as talking face to face. A conversation is so much more than words: a conversation is eyes, smiles, the silences between the words. When Stephie writes to her mother, her hand can't keep up with her mind, so it's difficult to get everything on paper; all the thoughts and feelings run through her head. And once the letter has been mailed, it can take several weeks before she gets an answer.

Aunt Märta never asks Stephie any questions or tells her any stories. She makes sure that Stephie does her homework, cleans her room, and helps with the housework. Nothing more.

In the evenings Aunt Märta sits in the front room and knits. At seven she turns on the radio to hear the news and the evening prayers. But the minute music comes on, she turns it off. "Secular" music is sinful, Aunt Märta tells Stephie, and secular music includes everything but hymns and spiritual songs like the ones the choir sings at the Pentecostal Church. Jazz, popular music, and classical music, it's all the same to Aunt Märta—the devil's playground.

Sometimes when Aunt Märta is out, Stephie turns on the radio. Except for those times, the white frame house is silent.

Things are different when Uncle Evert is home. He talks to Stephie, tells stories about things that happened on board the fishing boat, asks her about school, praises her progress with Swedish, and makes a joke of her mistakes.

89

"I'll take you out on the *Diana* next summer," he tells her. "I'll teach you to row the dinghy, too."

Summer is a long way off. Stephie won't be here then, though she doesn't tell Uncle Evert that. She's already been in Sweden three months. "Six months at the very most," her father promised.

But the letters from home no longer contain updates about entry visas, Amsterdam, or America. Her father writes that he and Mamma have moved to an even smaller room, and that Mamma now has a job keeping house for an older lady. Mamma, a housekeeper! Stephie can't imagine her mother wearing an apron and working in someone else's kitchen.

Mamma doesn't write anything about her work. Her letters are full of questions about Aunt Märta and Uncle Evert, about school, about whether Stephie is making friends on the island. Stephie answers that everyone is kind to her, that she has lots of friends and is doing well at school. The last part, at least, is true. She often even learns the verses of the hymns by heart, though she only just barely understands what they're about.

In every letter, Mamma asks Stephie to remind Nellie to write home.

You're the big sister, and I depend on you to help your little sister, Mamma writes. *Be sure she writes to us regularly, and try to help her keep up her German. Her spelling has become so much worse. Of course, I'm pleased that you're learning Swedish, but German is your mother tongue and one day you will be back.*

"Tomorrow," Nellie promises when Stephie tells her to

write home. "I'll do it tomorrow. Today I'm going to play with Sonja after school." Sonja is a friend from class.

But when the next day comes around, Nellie has plans to go to one of her classmates', or she's invited one of them back to Auntie Alma's. Nellie is popular. Every morning when she gets to school a flock of girls is waiting for her, competing to be her chosen playmate. Nellie laughs and jokes as if she's known Swedish her whole life.

No one waits in the schoolyard for Stephie. Vera sticks with Sylvia's gang, and Stephie's not welcome among them. She has to seek out Britta and her friends if she wants someone to play with. Although they let her join in when she asks, she always feels like an intruder. They talk so easily about people and things she knows nothing about. No one ever invites her home after school. Once, she tries to ask Britta back with her.

"It's too far," Britta answers. "I don't think my mother would let me. Not at this time of year when it's so dark."

The worst thing of all is Sylvia's constant teasing. Stephie's German accent, her clothes, her appearance—everything that makes her different from the others—is the object of Sylvia's ridicule, and she nosedives straight at her target like a seagull swooping down to pick up a juicy morsel.

"Horsehair," Sylvia says, pulling on one of Stephie's braids. "Look, her mane is braided! Why don't you wear feathers in it as well, like a circus horse?"

"Hee-hee-hee," Sylvia's crowd giggles. All but Vera, who just looks away and pretends not to hear.

Svante likes Stephie's braids. Sometimes he strokes one

furtively as he walks by her in the classroom. When he touches her, Stephie pulls back from his big hands, hands that are never completely clean.

Vera teases Svante, imitating his clumsy movements and the way he slurs his words. Vera is very good at imitation. She notices little details, gestures and expressions, and captures them perfectly.

Once, when Miss Bergström is out of the room, Vera imitates her. When the teacher returns with a map, the class is laughing loudly. They have to pinch one another to stop before there's trouble. Another time Vera waves her hands and rolls her *r*'s like the preacher at the Pentecostal Church, though it upsets Britta and the other children who go to Sunday school there.

Of course Svante's interest in Stephie hasn't passed Sylvia by unnoticed.

"The Princess from Vienna has an admirer," she says with a sneer. "The Princess and the village idiot, just like in the fairy tales. Except Svante's not likely to turn into a prince!"

One day Svante pulls a package out of his schoolbag and hands it to Stephie. This happens during lunch break, when everyone is eating sandwiches and drinking milk in the classroom. At first Stephie thinks Svante's offering her one of his sandwiches, which are wrapped in greasy brown paper.

"No, thank you," she declines politely. "I've got my own."

Svante laughs loudly. "It isn't a sandwich," he says. "It's a present. For you."

"Come on, open it," urges Britta, who sits next to her.

"Yes, open it," says Sylvia, leaning forward to get a better view. "We want to see what your admirer bought you."

"I'll open it at home," Stephie says, hurriedly pressing the package into her knapsack.

Svante gets angry. "Open it now!" he tells her. "I want to be there when you do."

Stephie can't avoid it, so she unwraps the greasy brown paper. The package contains a roughly hewn handmade frame.

"Turn it over," Svante orders her impatiently.

Stephie turns the frame to the front. There's a picture in the frame, a familiar face that glares at her. A face she's seen thousands of times, in newspapers, on posters, in shop windows back home in Vienna. Black hair brushed down over the forehead, a black moustache, sinister eyes. It's a blurry picture in black and white, probably from a magazine. A framed picture of Hitler.

"I made it myself," Svante tells her. "Do you like it?"

Stephie stares at the picture, trying to make sense of it.

She remembers seeing Hitler once in real life. It was last March, when the German army made a triumphal procession through the streets of Vienna. Hitler was there, chauffeured in a black Mercedes.

Stephie and Evi snuck out to watch the parade, against the instructions of their mothers. At first it seemed exciting—like a special occasion.

"Heil Hitler! Heil Hitler!"

People pushed and shoved to be able to see better. Lots of them raised their arms in the Nazi salute.

A fat woman shoved the girls aside. A uniformed man stared nastily at them. Stephie and Evi tried to push back through the crowd to get away, but they couldn't. In the end

93

they pressed up against the wall of a building, making themselves as invisible as they could, until the parade passed and the crowd began to disperse.

"Let me see," says Sylvia from the row behind. "What is it?"

She puts out a hand to take the picture from Stephie, who holds on to it, tight. In the tussle, Stephie knocks over her bottle of milk; the milk spills out over the picture and drips onto the floor.

"Don't you like it?" Svante asks in disappointment. "I thought you'd be pleased. You do come from Germany, don't you?"

He leans forward onto Stephie's desk, pressing his huge hands on the surface and bringing his pimply face right up to hers.

"Let me be," Stephie cries. "Leave me alone, you idiot!"

Miss Bergström appears in the doorway. "What on earth is going on here?" she asks.

"It's Stephie," Sylvia tells her. "Svante tried to give her a present, but she wouldn't accept it. She called him a stupid idiot."

"Stephanie," Miss Bergström says sharply. "That is not how we address one another at our school. Perhaps you do, where you come from. But we don't, here in Sweden."

Stephie rushes out of the classroom, down the stairs, and out into the schoolyard. She throws the picture to the ground, crushes it under her heel until that awful face is gone, and stamps on the frame until it breaks. Then she opens the door to the outhouse and tosses the whole thing into one of the holes, straight down into the smelly muck.

sixteen

"*But* you must understand that Svante didn't mean any harm," Britta says on their way home that day. "He can't help being stupid. Just imagine what it must be like to be repeating sixth grade for the second time and still not know your multiplication tables! He doesn't know anything about Hitler, either. I'm sure he honestly thought you'd be happy to get something that reminded you of home."

Stephie stops abruptly. "You're the one who doesn't see!" she screams at Britta. "You're just as stupid as Svante. You know nothing about it. Absolutely nothing at all!"

Britta looks offended. "But I do," she begins. "I know Hitler is evil. My father says so, but—"

"Your father doesn't know anything," Stephie interrupts. "My father's been in a labor camp, but you probably don't even know what that is."

She's not being fair, she knows that. So she doesn't wait for Britta to answer, just takes off, running along the side of the road at full speed.

"Wait!" Britta shouts after her. "Stephie, wait!"

She begins to run, too, catching up with Stephie just before she reaches the crossing where they go in separate directions.

"See you tomorrow," she says, "at Sunday school?"

"No."

"Jesus will be angry if you don't come," says Britta accusingly.

Stephie looks Britta right in the eye. "Jesus doesn't exist," Stephie says, putting all her father's authority into her voice. "He couldn't care less about me, or about you, or about anyone else, for that matter."

Britta blinks. Her bright eyes grow large, and tears well up in them. She takes a couple of steps back.

"Of course He exists," she cries. "Jesus lives and He loves me. But He doesn't care about you, because you're a vicious person. You're—you're not a real Christian!"

The minute Britta is out of sight over the top of the hill, Stephie wishes she'd behaved differently. Not because Britta's friendship is important to her. She's actually tired of Britta's endless know-it-all talk about Jesus. And she's tired of jumping rope, too.

But if she doesn't have Britta for a friend, then she's all alone. Alone at recess, alone walking back from school. And what if Britta tells her mother what Stephie said, and she tells Aunt Märta? Then Aunt Märta will realize Stephie hasn't really been redeemed. That she's only pretending to believe that Jesus is the son of God, which is kind of like lying. Maybe even worse.

Should she turn around and run after Britta? Tell her she didn't mean what she said and apologize? No, it's too late. Britta's house is just over the rise. Surely she's already home, sitting with her mother in the kitchen, telling her all about her school day. Telling her about Stephie, Svante, and the picture of Hitler. About their quarrel on the way home. About what Stephie said about Jesus. Britta's mother may already have lifted the receiver and asked the operator to connect her with Aunt Märta.

It begins to rain. Stephie passes Auntie Alma's house. She imagines the kitchen, warm and cozy. Nellie and the little ones are surely sitting around the table, eating sweet rolls hot out of the oven. In every single one of the houses she passes there are people, families of people talking to each other, caring about each other. She's the only one who's completely alone.

When the village houses are behind her, Stephie is unprotected from the wind. Gusts press the rain down on her, hard. She pushes into the wind, hands over her face to keep the drops off. When she gets to the thicket, it's not quite so bad, but then comes the long, open downhill path, and the wind takes her breath away.

She ought to run the last stretch toward home, hurry inside and take off her wet clothes, rub herself dry on one of Aunt Märta's rough linen towels until her skin stings. On cold, rainy days like today Aunt Märta usually has hot milk for her when she comes in from school.

Stephie passes the house right by and goes down to the

shore. The stones are wet and slippery. There are big heaps of rotting seaweed. Balancing awkwardly, she makes her way toward the thin strip of sand by the water's edge. A wave comes at her before she can pull back. Her stockings are soaked all the way up to the knee. Her shoes are full of water.

It's not good to have wet, cold feet. You can get pneumonia and die.

If she died, would anyone on the island except Nellie be sorry? she wonders. Who would write the news to her mother and father? Would Uncle Evert bury her here on the beach, like the sailor in a song Auntie Alma sometimes sings? When the sailor didn't come home as he'd promised, the girl he loved went down to the beach and drowned herself in the waves. The sailor had an anchor inscribed on her grave marker, instead of a crucifix.

The song is called "The Grave on the Beach." It isn't really a spiritual, but it is a very pretty, very sad song.

The water is black and icy cold today. It was probably summer when that girl drowned.

Stephie goes to the boathouse door and tugs at it. It isn't locked.

Inside are the scents of fish and pitch. Unfamiliar barrels and boxes line the walls.

Black fishnets are suspended on poles up near the ceiling. There's a broken oar, an old three-legged stool, and other objects Stephie can't quite distinguish in the dark. She finds a folded tarp, sits down on it, and unties her wet shoes. Then she pulls a corner of the tarp over herself and lies down. . . .

Someone is shaking her by the shoulder.

"Stephie," Uncle Evert's voice commands. "Come to, girl."

Stephie opens her eyes. Uncle Evert is leaning over her, slapping her cheeks gently. When he sees her eyes open, he stops.

"What in the world are you doing in here?" he asks. She can't tell if his tone is angry or concerned.

"I fell asleep," she answers foolishly. "I didn't mean to. I'm sorry."

"Wet as a drowned cat," Uncle Evert comments as he lifts the tarp off her. "Why on earth did you come to the boathouse?"

"I'm sorry," she repeats, though she's not really sure what she has to be sorry for.

Uncle Evert lifts her up and carries her all the way to the house, over the slippery stones and up the path.

"I can walk," Stephie tells him. "I'm not sick."

But she's glad Uncle Evert doesn't put her down. It feels safe just to be lying in his arms. When she was very little, before Nellie was born, her papa used to carry her in his arms when she was falling asleep. Gently she leans her head on Uncle Evert's shoulder.

"What in the world?" Aunt Märta asks, too, when Uncle Evert comes into the kitchen with Stephie and lays her on the wooden kitchen bench. "Where did you find her?"

"Lying in the boathouse," Uncle Evert tells her. "Did something happen?"

"Not that I know of," Aunt Märta replies. "Where are your shoes, Stephie?"

"I forgot them down there," she whispers. "I took them off. They were so wet."

"But what did you go to the boathouse for?" Uncle Evert asks. "Was somebody mean to you?"

"Yes," Stephie whispers. "Well, no, not exactly mean . . ."

That's all she can get out in Swedish.

"What a strange child," she hears Aunt Märta say while she is helping her out of her coat and sweater. Stephie's so cold she's shivering and her teeth are chattering.

"She'll have to have a hot bath," Aunt Märta continues. "You go into the front room, Evert."

Uncle Evert leaves the kitchen, shutting the door behind him. Aunt Märta heats water on the stove and pours it into the big tub. Stephie tries to unhook her stockings from her garters, but her fingers are too stiff. Aunt Märta has to help her.

The bathwater feels burning hot. As her cold body begins to thaw, her skin aches and prickles. She undoes her damp braids, letting her hair float on the surface of the water.

Aunt Märta brings towels and Stephie's nightgown. She helps Stephie dry her back, but leaves her to work through her snarled hair herself. Her mother used to comb it gently and part it down the middle. It's terribly knotted now: Stephie struggles with the comb. It hurts. She can't be bothered to unsnarl any more; she just brushes the top layer over the worst of the tangles.

100

Neither Uncle Evert nor Aunt Märta asks her any more questions. Stephie drinks hot milk with honey and goes to bed.

◊   ◊   ◊

The next morning she has a cold and is allowed to stay home from Sunday school. She ends up having to miss school the whole of the following week.

Uncle Evert stays home, too. There's a big storm, with winds so strong the *Diana* can't be at sea. Uncle Evert amuses Stephie with seamen's tales, and plays tic-tac-toe with her.

She stiffens every time the telephone rings, but it's never Britta's mother calling.

seventeen

*B*y the time Stephie is well enough to go back to school, it's snowing. Big, wet flakes fall to the ground and melt.

Svante doesn't touch her braids. That's something, anyway.

At recess, Britta takes Stephie aside. Stephie can tell from the look on her face that she has something important to say but that she's trying to drag out the suspense for as long as possible.

Stephie watches the snowflakes whirl. She has no intention of asking Britta what's on her mind. If Britta has something to say, let her come out with it.

Britta clears her throat. "I have decided to forgive you," she says solemnly. "If you honestly repent. I'm sure if you do, Jesus will forgive you, too."

"Thank you," says Stephie, trying to look repentant.

"Mamma says we must judge kindly and show forbearance," Britta goes on. "You have lived your whole life in the Kingdom of Sin. It's not your fault."

The Kingdom of Sin! Stephie opens her mouth to protest, but Britta continues.

"I want to help you find the true way," she says. "May I come home with you after school?"

"I'm not sure . . . ," Stephie falters.

"My mother's already asked your aunt," Britta says. "It's all right with her."

"Oh," Stephie mumbles. Things have been going on behind her back, but she can't figure out what.

After school they walk to Aunt Märta's together. Britta chatters about Sunday school, about the new song they learned when Stephie was absent, about the approaching holiday season, beginning with Lucia.

"What's Lucia?" Stephie asks.

"Don't you know?" Britta responds in surprise. "That's when we celebrate the Queen of Light."

This answer doesn't tell Stephie very much.

"Who's the Queen of Light?"

Britta explains excitedly all the details of the festival of Lucia.

"One girl in the class is elected Lucia. And six others are her handmaidens. Everybody votes."

"Who will it be?"

"Someone pretty," Britta says, and Stephie notes a tiny sigh. "And with a good singing voice."

Vera has a good voice. And she's pretty, too.

"We always choose Sylvia," Britta tells her.

They're on the last uphill. Britta's lagging behind. "Slow down, I've got a stitch in my side," she complains.

Suddenly Stephie has the urge to tease Britta. Instead of slowing down she speeds up.

"Wait up!" Britta shouts.

Stephie doesn't stop until she reaches the crest of the hill. She gazes out at the ocean. In the distance there's the blinking of a lighthouse. She sees a white flashing light, and if she steps to the side she can see a red one, too. Uncle Evert has explained to her that the boats have to follow the white light. If they're off course they see the red one, a warning against heading toward the cliffs and the shallows.

Britta catches up. "Why didn't you wait?" she asks reproachfully.

"I am waiting," Stephie retorts.

Britta's eyes narrow in annoyance, but then she appears to remember she is supposed to show forbearance.

"Is that the house down there?" she asks, her voice milder.

"The end of the world," Stephie says. But Britta doesn't seem to understand.

"They're wealthy, aren't they?" she asks. "The Janssons."

Stephie's never thought of Aunt Märta and Uncle Evert as wealthy before. Yes, they do have everything they need. But Aunt Märta does all the housework herself, with no housemaid, and Uncle Evert wears work clothes and smells of fish even when he's been home for several days.

"Not especially," Stephie replies.

"What about your family in Vienna?" Britta asks. "They're rich, aren't they?"

Stephie remembers the large apartment, the beautiful furniture, the soft rugs. She remembers her mother's elegant clothes, her fur coats and hats. And Papa's study with floor-to-ceiling bookshelves, filled with leather-bound volumes. She remembers all the things they had to leave behind when the Nazis took their apartment and her father's medical practice away from them.

"Not anymore," she answers curtly.

◇   ◇   ◇

Aunt Märta is waiting for them, and she opens the front door as they arrive.

"How nice to see you, Britta," she says. "Come in."

As they hang up their coats, Aunt Märta asks Britta how her mother is, how her grandmother is, and other questions about people Stephie has never heard of. Britta answers politely.

"Now you may show Britta your room," Aunt Märta tells Stephie. "I'll bring you sweet rolls and fruit drink in a while."

Stephie leads Britta up the stairs.

Britta looks at Stephie's room, nodding in recognition at the picture of Jesus, and pointing at the photos on the dresser.

"Are those your parents?"

"Yes."

Britta looks briefly at the portrait of Papa, and then spends a long time studying Mamma. For an instant, Stephie sees her mother through Britta's eyes. Her permed hair, her

105

lipsticked lips, the elegant fur stole around her neck. So unlike the women on the island with their tightly twisted buns, their plain faces and cotton dresses.

She can imagine what Britta is thinking about Mamma: shallow and vain. Sinful. Like the film stars in the magazines Sylvia sometimes brings to school to show the other girls.

It's not true, Stephie wants to say. *Mamma's not like that. Since when is it a crime to be beautiful, anyway?*

In her mind's eye she sees her mother's face as it looked that morning at the train station, the morning of Stephie and Nellie's departure. Mamma's red lips made her face look even paler, and Stephie noticed taut little lines around her mouth she had never seen before. Mamma had been up almost all night packing, having second thoughts and repacking. When they left she forgot the sandwiches she'd made, and they had to go back and get them.

"What other things do you have with you from Vienna?" Britta asks.

Stephie opens the bottom drawer of her dresser and removes her treasures. Britta tries the fountain pen and looks curiously at Stephie's diary. Stephie doesn't mind, it's in German. Britta admires the dancing ballerina and tries on Stephie's jewelry. Then she catches sight of the balled-up handkerchief at the back of the drawer.

"What's that?" she asks, and before Stephie can answer she has reached in and pulled out the little ball.

"Give it to me," Stephie says.

"Let me just take a peek," Britta insists, taking a step back from Stephie's outstretched hand.

106

"No, leave it alone."

Stephie grabs Britta by the arm just as Britta opens the handkerchief. And just as Aunt Märta appears in the doorway, carrying a tray. Mimi, the china dog, rolls out of Britta's hand and shatters on the floor.

"Oh, I'm so sorry," Britta begins. "I didn't break it on purpose."

But Aunt Märta lift's Mimi's head up off the floor.

"What is this?" she asks sharply. "Is it yours?"

"It wasn't my fault," Britta whines shrilly. "I just wanted to look at it."

"Alma has a dog like this," Aunt Märta says. "Is this hers? Did you take it from her?" she asks Stephie.

Stephie stares down at what is left of Mimi. A leg, a tail, the base of the figure. Plus lots of little chips, too small to glue back together.

"Did you?"

"Yes," Stephie whispers. "But I meant to put it back."

"That makes you a thief." Aunt Märta's voice sounds like the snapping of a whip.

"I'm going home now," Britta says.

"Yes, I think you'd better," Aunt Märta confirms. "Stephie, you get the broom and dustpan and clean up in here. Then you will go see Auntie Alma and apologize."

Aunt Märta sees Britta to the door. Stephie gets the broom and dustpan, sweeps up the bits and pieces of china, and carries them down to the rubbish pail.

eighteen

Aunt Märta has a long phone conversation with Auntie Alma. Stephie sits on her bed awaiting judgment. Will she have to walk all the way to Auntie Alma's and back in the dark? Will she be punished?

Aunt Märta's eagle eyes find a tiny sliver of china on the floor that Stephie missed.

"Pick that up," she commands.

Stephie picks up the sliver obediently. It's so small she can just barely grip it between her thumb and index finger.

"Auntie Alma and I have agreed that you won't go over there this evening," she tells Stephie. "You need time to reflect upon what you have done and sincerely regret it. After Sunday school this weekend you will accompany Nellie to Auntie Alma's and ask forgiveness."

At first Stephie is relieved. But as the hours pass she

begins to feel that it would have been better to just get it over with. It's only Wednesday. There are four days until Sunday. Four long days.

The next morning Britta turns her back on Stephie in the school hallway and sits at the far edge of the bench they share in class. It's as if Stephie has some contagious disease.

"Today we're going to elect this year's Lucia," Miss Bergström tells the class. "Are there any nominations?"

Barbro raises her hand eagerly.

"Barbro?"

"I nominate Sylvia as our Lucia."

"Any other nominations?"

The class is silent. No other hands are raised.

"Are you certain?"

Margit, a small girl who sometimes jumps rope with Britta, raises a hand shyly.

"Margit?"

"Sylvia," she more or less whispers.

"Sylvia has already been nominated," Miss Bergström replies." "No other names, then?"

"Yes, please," Stephie says.

"In this class we raise our hands if we wish to speak," Miss Bergström scolds. "Yes?"

"Vera," says Stephie. "I nominate Vera to be Lucia."

There's a giggle. A pen drops to the floor. Vera turns around and glares strangely at Stephie. Sylvia cocks her head, a smile glued to her lips.

"All right," Miss Bergström tells the class. "We'll have to vote, then."

Vera raises her hand. "I don't want to be Lucia," she says. "Sylvia fits the part much better than me."

"That will be up to the class to decide," Miss Bergström declares, giving Ingrid, the class monitor, pieces of paper to pass out. Each pupil is supposed to take one, write the name of the person he or she votes for, and fold it in half. Miss Bergström writes Sylvia's and Vera's names at the top of the blackboard.

When everyone has voted, Ingrid collects the ballots and gives them to Miss Bergström. The teacher unfolds the first one.

"Vera," she says, making a vertical mark under Vera's name on the board.

Stephie wonders if that was her ballot. Will hers be the only vote in favor of Vera?

"Vera," says Miss Bergström again, making a new mark on the board. "Vera. Vera."

One ballot after the next, one mark after the next under Vera's name. Hardly any under Sylvia's.

"Vera. Vera. Vera. Sylvia."

When the votes have all been counted, Vera has twenty-six votes and Sylvia only five.

"A redheaded Lucia," Sylvia says loudly, without raising her hand. "Well, that'll be a first!"

"All right, then, Vera," says Miss Bergström. "You will be the class Lucia this year."

Vera looks miserable. "My gown's too short," she says.

"Let the hem down," says Miss Bergström. "Or add some lace edging if need be. There's a crown you can borrow, of course."

"We won't need any candles," Barbro says. "Her hair's already in flames."

"What's got into all of you today?" Miss Bergström scolds. "The next person who speaks without raising a hand will be sent out to stand in the hall. Sylvia will be one of the handmaidens. Understood?"

The class mumbles agreement.

"I have one more suggestion," Miss Bergström continues. "Stephanie has never celebrated Lucia before. In fact, this may be her only opportunity. I propose we let her be a handmaiden as well."

No one says anything. No objections, no support.

The class elects the other handmaidens: Barbro, Gunvor, Majbritt, and Ingrid. Plus Sylvia and Stephie. Except for Ingrid, all the others are part of Sylvia's crowd.

When recess begins Miss Bergström asks Stephie to stay behind.

"You'll need a long white cotton gown," she tells her. "Ask your foster mother to get you one. And a green wreath for your head. Crowberry greens will do, we have so few lingonberry bushes on the island."

In the schoolyard Stephie looks for Vera, but she's nowhere to be seen. Sylvia glares at Stephie and whispers with her friends.

"I'll get you back for this," she says into Stephie's ear on their way up the stairs.

The day passes slowly. Stephie has trouble concentrating, and is reprimanded by Miss Bergström. She tries to focus on King Karl XII going to war with Russia. But the broken china dog and the prospect of apologizing to Auntie

111

Alma preoccupy her. So, too, do Vera's strange expression, Sylvia's threat, and the white cotton gown she somehow has to get. She barely hears Miss Bergström talking.

"Stephanie?" Her own name penetrates the fog of her thoughts.

"Excuse me?" she mumbles.

Miss Bergström lets Britta answer the question. She always knows the answer to things you can learn by heart—verses of hymns, dates when things happened, names of mountain peaks and capital cities.

The last hour of the day they have dictation. This is Stephie's least favorite subject in Swedish school. Although she has learned to speak reasonably well, she finds it almost impossible to master the spelling.

"The ship's captain had already embarked," Miss Bergström reads, "and they headed out to sea to intercept the drifting vessel . . ."

Stephie dips her pen in the inkwell and writes. She stops. How do you spell "intercept"?

". . . to intersept the drifting vessel," she writes.

". . . zigzagging between the giant waves," Miss Bergström continues.

She must have missed something. What could it have been? Stephie thinks hard, trying to re-create the missing words. Now she's forgotten what Miss Bergström has just read.

"Stephanie," Miss Bergström says. "Why aren't you writing?"

"I don't know the words."

"What's the trouble with you today?" Miss Bergström asks impatiently. "Are you ill again?"

Stephie shakes her head and instantly wishes she hadn't. She could have said she felt as if she had a temperature. Then she would have been sent home.

"Keep at it, then," Miss Bergström scolds, continuing the dictation. Stephie picks up her pen. The words continue to misbehave. At last the bell rings.

She walks home alone. Britta hasn't said a word to her all day.

Down the road she sees a head of red hair. She picks up speed and catches up with Vera. She can't imagine her being anything but pleased to have been chosen to be Lucia.

Vera rebukes her angrily. "What did you go and do that for?" she wants to know.

"What?"

"Don't stick your nose into places where it has no business!" Vera says sharply. "Sylvia's never going to forgive me."

"You? I'm the one she's angry at."

"You just don't get it," Vera screams. "Idiot! You've ruined everything."

"I didn't mean . . . ," Stephie begins, but Vera isn't listening. She takes a turn in the road and disappears, her red hair shimmering behind her.

nineteen

"*Will* they send you home now, Stephie?" Nellie asks once they leave Sunday school.

"No," Stephie says. "We can't go home. There's a war on, stupid."

They can't send her back to Vienna, no matter what she does. But maybe they can send her somewhere else. To a different family, or an orphanage. A new place where she won't even have Nellie.

Nellie is quiet. When they get to Auntie Alma's, she tries to be comforting.

"Well, if they send you home, at least you'll get to be with Mamma and Papa." She opens the front door and shouts, "Mother, here we are!"

Mother! Is Nellie calling Auntie Alma *mother* now? Stephie goes hot with rage.

114

"Auntie Alma's not your mother," she begins, but that's all there's time to say before Auntie Alma walks into the hall.

She ushers Stephie into the front room, closing the door behind them, and sits down at the table.

Stephie's on the edge of her chair, holding one hand on each side of the seat, as if afraid she's going to fall off. She can hear Nellie and the little ones in the kitchen.

"Why did you take it?" Auntie Alma begins. Her voice has a sharp tone Stephie's never heard before.

"I'm sorry," Stephie whispers. "I'm so terribly sorry it broke."

"I don't mind about the dog," Auntie Alma explains. "What I'm upset about is that you took it without asking. Don't you know that's stealing?"

"I meant to put it back," Stephie says so softly she's almost breathing the words.

"But it's wrong to take things that belong to others," Auntie Alma goes on. " 'Thou shalt not steal.' Haven't you learned that at Sunday school?"

"I already knew it," Stephie says in a louder, more defiant tone. Auntie Alma must think she never learned anything at home. As if the Ten Commandments had been invented by these islanders.

"I'm disappointed in you," Auntie Alma tells her. "I've always stood up for you until now." She sounds offended, as if she thinks Stephie took the dog just to make her feel bad. "Why did you do it?"

Stephie doesn't say anything. Auntie Alma glares at her sternly.

115

After some time Stephie speaks up. "I just wanted to hold it," she says.

Auntie Alma sighs.

"I regret it," Stephie says. "I truly repent. I will never do anything like that again. Please forgive me, Auntie Alma."

At those words Auntie Alma smiles and pats Stephie on the cheek.

"Good girl," she says. "I forgive you. As long as you are truly repentant."

But that's not the end of it. That evening there is a prayer meeting at the Pentecostal Church. Stephie has to go along with Aunt Märta; it doesn't help that she was at Sunday school just that very morning. At the meeting, Aunt Märta instructs her to kneel down.

"We must pray together," she says.

Aunt Märta begins to pray out loud, in her powerful voice. She prays for Jesus to guide Stephie on the true path and to help her refrain from sin. Stephie's cheeks are on fire. She peeks out of the corner of her eye to see whether others are listening.

"Pray," Aunt Märta commands, nudging her in the side.

"Dear Jesus," Stephie begins, but then doesn't know how to go on. "Dear Jesus, help me not to be a bad girl. Make me good. And make Sylvia nicer, too. And let me soon be with Mamma and Papa again."

"Pray for forgiveness," Aunt Märta whispers.

"And forgive me for taking Mimi from Auntie Alma's cupboard."

"Mimi? What kind of foolish talk is that?" Aunt Märta

scolds as they are leaving the meeting. "Names are a privilege reserved for the living. And boats, of course."

Stephie keeps quiet. She's thinking about a real little dog named Mimi. A little dog with brown patches in her white fur and a damp, black nose.

Before she goes to bed she gets her knapsack ready for school the next day. There's a piece of paper with the text to the song for Lucia. She has to know it by heart before Wednesday, Lucia Day. It's a difficult melody, but she plans to sing softly, and mouth the words.

It's Sunday, and she still hasn't spoken to Aunt Märta about the white gown she needs. Soon it will be too late. Aunt Märta probably won't want to go all the way to Göteborg to get one. Will there be one she can borrow? Or could they make one?

Aunt Märta's in the rocking chair, reading the newspaper.

"Excuse me," Stephie begins. "It's Lucia Day on Wednesday."

Aunt Märta looks up. "Is it?" she replies.

"I'm going to be one of the handmaidens."

Aunt Märta nods. "That's nice." She turns the page.

Stephie gathers her courage. "I'll need a long white gown."

"I'm sure that can be arranged," Aunt Märta says in a voice that is almost gentle. "Off to bed with you, now."

The evening before Lucia Day Stephie finds a folded, neatly ironed garment on her bed. She unfolds it. It's a long, cotton flannel nightgown that buttons all the way up.

White, but with a faded pattern of little blue flowers still slightly visible.

Stephie had imagined a Lucia gown as different, prettier, with lace and ribbons like a wedding dress. But Aunt Märta must know best. Stephie folds it back up neatly, wraps it in tissue paper, and packs it in her schoolbag.

The next morning she leaves a whole hour earlier than usual. They're going to rehearse the Lucia performance before the rest of the class arrives. It's snowy and windy—an easterly wind for once, so it's against her as she walks to school.

Miss Bergström has already let the other children in. The girls are getting ready in the classroom, while two boys who are participating change in the map room down the hall.

Vera has on a simple white gown with a little round collar. Miss Bergström is tying a wide red silk sash around her waist. Sylvia is twirling around, showing off her lovely cotton gown with wide lace edging on the collar and sleeves.

Ingrid, the class monitor, is changing in the corner. She, too, is pulling a completely white cotton gown over her head. All the girls have solid white gowns.

Stephie goes over by Ingrid and starts changing. She shivers with the cold, hurrying to remove Aunt Märta's flannel gown from her schoolbag. Ingrid, peeking out of the corner of her eye, does a double take.

Stephie pulls the gown over her head and starts buttoning all the little buttons. The sleeves are a bit too long and keep getting in her way.

"Look," Barbro calls out. "Look at Stephie!"

118

Everyone looks. Sylvia bursts into loud laughter.

"She's just got an old nightgown!"

"Flowered!" Barbro snorts.

Gunvor and Majbritt join in the laughter. Ingrid looks toward Miss Bergström and laughs behind her hand. Vera, pale and nervous, doesn't seem to notice what's going on. And she isn't laughing.

"Quiet," Miss Bergström shouts. "Stop, this very instant."

"She can't wear that, can she?" Sylvia asks. "It will ruin the whole Lucia procession. It's bad enough she can't sing."

Miss Bergström sighs. "Just wait here," the teacher says. "I'll organize a different gown. Ingrid, you keep everyone in order, please."

It feels as if Miss Bergström's gone for a very long time, though it's probably no longer than ten minutes. Stephie removes the nightgown and pulls on her cardigan over her undergarments so she won't freeze. The other girls brush their hair and gossip in whispers. Vera repeats the Lucia verses over and over again.

"We're not going to have much time to rehearse now," Ingrid complains.

"Right," Sylvia agrees. "And whose fault is that?"

Finally Miss Bergström reappears with a gown. It's too short for Stephie, but Miss Bergström lets down the hem.

"No one will notice," she tells Stephie. "But you'll have to take it home and hem it back up. I borrowed it from the caretaker's wife. It's too small for her daughter this year."

They rehearse the songs a couple of times. Then they stand waiting in the map room.

"Now," Miss Bergström says, opening the door to the

hall. She lights the six candles in Vera's heavy crown. The handmaidens each carry a lit candle between their clasped hands. Slowly the group walks down the hallway, where the rest of the class is lining the walls, watching. Stephie and Ingrid are right behind Vera, with Sylvia and Barbro next, followed by Gunvor and Majbritt and, last of all, the two boys, dressed in long white robes and pointed hats topped with gold stars.

They are nearly at the classroom door when Stephie feels a hand grab one of her braids. She hardly has time to react before she hears a hissing sound and smells a nasty, burnt odor.

"Fire!" someone shouts.

Stephie has her right braid in her hand now and is staring at it. All the hair below the rubber band is singed, leaving only scorched ends.

"What on earth happened here?" Miss Bergström asks.

"I don't know," says Sylvia innocently. "Stephie must have tossed her head and her braid touched my candle. Or Barbro's."

"Right," Barbro agrees. "That must be what happened."

Stephie says nothing. Sylvia is her enemy, and she's stronger than Stephie.

twenty

The big scissors from the kitchen drawer rest heavily in Stephie's hand. She lifts her scorched braid and looks at it. The burnt ends reek.

The house is silent. She's all alone.

She tests the scissors on the hair just below the rubber band holding her braid tight. Then she raises the scissors a little higher up, and higher again, until they graze her neck.

In the mirror over the washbasin, Stephie's face is pale. She looks herself straight in the eyes and cuts.

The sharp edges eat their way into the thick braid. Stephie tightens her grip until the blades meet with a firm clink.

Her cut-off braid hangs loose in her hand like a dead snake. Looking into the mirror again, Stephie sees a strange sight. Half her face looks like the Stephie she knows, the other like a strange creature with wild black hair sticking out every which way.

She hears the front door open and shut.

"Stephie," Aunt Märta calls, "are you home?"

"Yes," she calls back, never taking her eyes off the mirror.

"What are you doing?"

"Nothing much."

"You've got mail," Aunt Märta says.

Braid in hand, Stephie goes downstairs. Aunt Märta stares at her.

"What have you done, girl? Have you lost your mind?"

"I only meant to cut off a little," Stephie tells her. "I don't know how it happened."

"Ah, well," says Aunt Märta. "Short hair's very practical, really."

Stephie sits on a chair in the kitchen with an old towel around her neck. Aunt Märta unbraids the other side of her hair and cuts it all to an even length. Big tufts fall onto the newspapers Aunt Märta has spread out on the floor.

Then Aunt Märta gets smaller scissors from her mending basket and evens off the ends. Stephie shuts her eyes. She can hardly believe the hands so gently and carefully touching her hair are the rough hands she knows as Aunt Märta's.

When Aunt Märta is done, Stephie goes to the hall mirror to have a look. Her hair doesn't look funny now, but she barely recognizes herself. Her neck appears to be long and thin and her eyes look larger. The weight of the braids she always felt when she moved her head is gone. She feels naked.

Aunt Märta passes by with her cut-off braid, throwing it and the rest of the hair into the rubbish pail. When Stephie sees her braid lying among potato peels and fish bones, she wishes she had saved it. But it's too late now.

After Stephie has cleaned up the newspaper and swept the loose strands of hair off the floor, Aunt Märta opens her bag and gives her two letters.

One has a German stamp and Papa's handwriting on the envelope. The other is postmarked in Göteborg and bears the return address of the Swedish relief committee.

Stephie's heart is pounding. It must mean something that these two letters arrived on the same day. Just think if everything is arranged! Just think if Mamma and Papa have their entry visas for America!

Aunt Märta pulls the letter opener through the flap on the envelope from the Swedish relief committee, even though it's addressed to Stephie.

The letter is typed. The ribbon must be old, because some words are blurry. It begins with the word "Dear" followed by a handwritten "Stephanie."

"Dear Stephanie," Aunt Märta reads aloud. "The relief committee wishes you a Merry Christmas and hopes that you feel at home in Sweden now."

Aunt Märta straightens her reading glasses, glancing at Stephie over the top. Stephie nods eagerly. All right, she feels at home. Anything to make Aunt Märta keep reading. She wishes she could just grab the letter and read it herself. Does it or does it not contain the message she is hoping for?

". . . be obedient to your foster parents and grateful to them for having taken you in. . . . Try your best to improve your Swedish. . . . Learn from your Swedish friends."

With every sentence Aunt Märta reads, Stephanie loses more and more hope. If she were going to be leaving soon, such admonitions would be unnecessary. Yet she listens impatiently until the very end, just in case the words she longs to hear are there after all.

"Never forget," Aunt Märta reads, "that ungrateful, lazy children do a great disservice not only to themselves but also to our work as a whole, and to all the Jews."

Aunt Märta puts the letter down.

"Is that all?" Stephie asks.

Aunt Märta nods. "Except 'Our very best wishes' and the signature."

She pushes the letter across the table. Stephie picks it up and glances quickly through it. Nothing but admonitions.

"Wise counsel," Aunt Märta says. "I hope you'll take those words to heart. Save the letter and reread it now and then."

Stephie folds the letter and closes the envelope. She intends never to open it again.

After dinner she goes up to her room and shuts the door. With trembling hands she opens Papa's letter. Perhaps he and Mamma have gotten their entry visas after all, but the relief committee ladies don't know.

There are two sheets of paper in the envelope. One is in her father's handwriting, the other in her mother's.

My sweet Stephie, Papa writes. *When you and Nellie left, we believed we would be apart only for a short while. Now four months have passed and it seems that we will not be reunited for some time. In spite of all my efforts, we have not been granted entry permits to America. The future looks bleak, but we must not give up hope.*

"Not give up hope." Where is Stephie supposed to get hope from, when all she ever feels is disappointment? The tears in her eyes make Papa's handwriting go blurry. She wipes them away and continues reading. Papa writes that he is now being allowed to work at the Jewish Hospital.

It is very tiring, because there are so few of us and so little equipment and medicine. But this is my only opportunity to work as a doctor, and every single day I am aware how sorely my services are needed.

Dearest Stephie, you are a big girl and must be brave. Take care of Nellie, she's younger and cannot be expected to understand things as well as you. We must all continue to see this as a passing situation, and believe that we will soon be together again. It is a great comfort to your mother and me to know that you two are safe, whatever happens.

Her father's letter ends with best regards to Stephie's "Swedish family." *Please tell them how grateful Mamma and I are that they are taking care of you,* he writes. Grateful, grateful, and more grateful!

She puts down the sheet of paper with its tiny handwriting and opens the letter from her mother.

My dear one! I miss you and Nellie so. Every day I look at your framed photographs and at the picture from our picnic in the Wienerwald. But the pictures are old now and you have surely grown in the salt sea air. I would so much appreciate receiving new photos. Has anyone taken your pictures recently? Perhaps

125

with your Swedish families in them, too? Please send any you might have! If you have none, perhaps you could ask someone with a camera to take your pictures? Tell them your mother so badly wants to see what you look like after four months in Sweden.

Stephie's hand flies to her neck, touching her hair and the naked flesh below it. What will Mamma say when she sees Stephie without her braids? She used to love them so.

Last summer, when they'd first arrived, Auntie Alma took some pictures of Stephie and Nellie playing with Elsa and John. Perhaps Stephie could send them to Mamma and say there are no more recent ones.

Sooner or later Mamma will find out. But hair grows faster after it's cut. Perhaps it will be back down to her shoulders by the time they get to America.

twenty-one

Sylvia sneers when she sees Stephie's hair.

"Goodness, did your whole mane burn up?"

"No, she must've chopped it off with sheep shears," Barbro comments.

Stephie doesn't reply. Back home she was good at defending herself with words. Whenever anyone said something nasty to her, she would make a quick retort. But in Swedish her words come out so slowly and are so insufficient. She just turns away.

After the end-of-term program Stephie walks home, filled with good feelings from the beautiful Christmas music and all the candles.

"Lo, how a rose e'er blooming . . . ," she hums to herself, almost unaware of Nellie's presence beside her and of what her sister is talking about.

"Sonja gave me a Christmas present," Nellie boasts. "But I mustn't open it until Christmas Eve. And Auntie Alma's going to take our pictures today, too. I'm going to send one to Mamma for Christmas."

Stephie stops in mid-step. "Who told you that?"

"Mamma wrote that she wanted one," Nellie replies. "Didn't she write and ask you, too?"

"No," Stephie lies.

"Oh, well, she asked me," Nellie says. "So I'll buy a frame when we go into Göteborg to do our Christmas shopping. We're going to a pastry shop, too."

"There are no pastry shops in Göteborg," Stephie asserts. "No real ones, anyhow, like in Vienna."

"Oh, yes there are."

That's when Stephie notices that Nellie is answering her in Swedish, although Stephie has been speaking German.

"Why are you speaking Swedish with me?"

"Why shouldn't I?"

"Because we speak German, that's our language."

"It sounds so stupid," Nellie says. "If anybody else hears."

"So do you think you're Swedish now, or something?"

Nellie doesn't say anything, just takes a wrapped present out of her pocket and rattles it near her ear.

"Mamma and Papa would be upset if they heard you," Stephie tells her. "Very upset and angry."

Nellie thrusts the present back in her pocket. She sticks out her bottom lip and doesn't say another word the rest of the way to the house.

Auntie Alma has set the table and prepared raspberry

juice, saffron buns, and ginger cookies. She asks to see their report cards and praises them for having worked so hard.

"Before you know it you'll both be best in your class," she tells them. "As soon as you've really mastered Swedish."

"I think we'll get our next report cards in American English," Stephie tells her. "If our English is good enough by then."

Auntie Alma's forehead creases. "Oh, my dear," she tells Stephie, "I don't think you ought to count on being able to travel to America this spring."

"But," Stephie begins, "Father wrote . . ."

Elsa and John are tired of sitting still. They leave the table and start chasing each other around the kitchen, shouting loudly. Nellie slides off her chair, too, catching John in her arms. She tickles him and he laughs so hard he's near tears.

"I don't doubt that your father is doing his very best," Auntie Alma continues. "But travel is not easy when there's a war on."

What is Auntie Alma trying to tell her? Will they be staying on the island all the way to the end of the war? How long is that going to be?

"But America . . . ," Stephie begins. "America's not involved in the war."

Auntie Alma is busy with the children and has stopped listening.

"Don't forget you've got your good clothes on," she scolds them. "We're going to have our pictures taken today, you know."

That, too. Stephie had nearly forgotten.

"Do we have to get new pictures?" Stephie asks. "Can't we send the ones you took last summer, Auntie Alma?"

"No, Nellie's told me your mamma asked for more recent pictures. And since you're dressed up today, it's the perfect opportunity."

Auntie Alma takes their picture on the steps in front of the house. First Stephie and Nellie alone, then all four children.

"Now you take one with me in it, too," Auntie Alma tells Stephie.

"I don't know how."

"It's easy," Auntie Alma replies. "I'll set the focus and distance, and all you have to do is click the shutter."

Auntie Alma shows Stephie where to stand and which button to press. She goes over to the steps, holding John in her arms. The little girls stand one on either side of her. Stephie holds the camera as steady as she can. There's a little metallic click when she presses the shutter release.

"I'll leave the film in Göteborg to be developed," Auntie Alma says. "Sigurd can pick it up after Christmas."

Nellie looks disappointed. "I thought it would be my Christmas present to Mamma," she whines.

"No, dummy," Stephie says to her. "Not even a regular letter would get to Vienna before Christmas if you mailed it now."

Nellie sticks her tongue out at her sister. "Know-it-all," she says.

Stephie helps Auntie Alma clean up in the kitchen, hoping the whole time that Auntie Alma will invite her to join them on their outing to Göteborg. But Auntie Alma just chatters on, and Stephie can't get herself to ask if she may come along.

Nellie walks Stephie to the gate when it's time for her to go.

"Stephie?" she begins.

"What?"

"I'd like to buy Sonja a Christmas present, since she gave me one."

"Do," Stephie replies. "Buy her something in Göteborg."

Nellie shakes her head. "Auntie Alma promised me enough money to buy the frame for Mamma and something for you. There won't be enough for Sonja, too. Do you have any money?"

Stephie has the coin the sailor tossed her that day so long ago, and another Uncle Evert gave her. But she doesn't want to give all her money to Nellie to spend on a present for Sonja, who she thinks is a pesky little girl.

"I need the money I have for my own Christmas shopping," she says.

"What should I do, then?"

Stephie shrugs. "How should I know? Ask Auntie Alma for more money."

"I can't do that."

"So don't buy anything for Sonja."

"But Sonja's my best friend. She's the nicest girl in my class. And I'm sure she got me a really special present."

"Give her something of yours," Stephie suggests. "One of the things you brought from home."

"Like what?"

Stephie answers without thinking. The words just pop out: "Your coral necklace."

Nellie blanches. "Oh, I could never give that away. It's Mamma's."

"No, she gave it to you."

"Do you really think I should?" Nellie's voice trembles slightly. "Give it away?"

"Yes," Stephie tells her. "Unless you've got something else."

Nellie shakes her head.

"Do whatever you think best," Stephie concludes. "Goodbye."

After walking a short distance, she turns around. Nellie's still at the gate. She looks so little. Stephie wants to go back and tell her she didn't mean it about the necklace. But somehow she just keeps walking.

Nellie would never really do it, she thinks. *Never.*

twenty-two

The week before Christmas, Aunt Märta and Stephie clean the house from top to bottom. They hang handwoven Christmas motifs on the kitchen walls and put an embroidered tablecloth with elves and evergreen boughs on the table in the front room. Aunt Märta bakes bread and prepares a ham.

When it's time to marinate the herring, Aunt Märta discovers she's out of vinegar.

"You can go to the shop for me," she tells Stephie. "Don't dawdle, I need it right away."

Stephie leaves, a big canvas bag over her arm, a shopping list and Aunt Märta's coin purse in the right-hand pocket of her coat. She has her own money, her two coins, in the left-hand pocket. She plans on buying her Christmas presents for Nellie and Uncle Evert.

She's giving Aunt Märta a pot holder she crocheted in sewing class. It's a little uneven and has some holes, but after Stephie had undone and redone her work three times, the crafts teacher said it would have to do.

Every time anyone opens or closes the shop door a little bell rings. The shopkeeper is behind the counter, measuring coffee into brown paper bags. The shelves behind him are full of cans, bottles, and boxes. On the floor there's a wooden barrel of herring, along with huge sacks of flour, sugar, and coffee beans. On the counter stand tempting glass jars full of soft and hard candy.

Stephie's the only customer.

"Good day," she greets the shopkeeper politely. He nods curtly and goes on weighing the bags of coffee.

Stephie waits. The shopkeeper pays her no attention until he has filled and closed all the bags in front of him.

"All right. What do you need?"

Stephie pulls out her shopping list and begins to read: "A bottle of vinegar, a pound of coffee, two pounds of oat . . ."

The shopkeeper takes a bottle of vinegar down from the shelf behind him and sets it on the counter. Next to it he places one of the bags of coffee.

The door opens.

"What can I do for you, ma'am?" the shopkeeper says, turning to the woman who comes in.

". . . meal," Stephie continues. Then she falls silent.

The woman has a long shopping list. She samples several cheeses before deciding, then pinches and pokes at least twenty oranges before choosing four. Stephie shifts from one foot to the other impatiently. She knows Aunt Märta is waiting for the vinegar.

Sylvia comes strolling down the stairs. She leans forward, arms on the counter, chin in her hands.

"My Christmas dress is blue," she says. "What color is yours?"

Stephie doesn't answer.

"Aren't you getting a new dress to wear on Christmas?"

"Sure," Stephie lies. "But it's going to be a surprise."

Sylvia smiles her superior smile. "I don't believe you."

Finally the lady's got everything on her list and is paying. Sylvia settles in on a stool in the corner behind the counter, leafing through a magazine.

"Thank you," the shopkeeper says. "Thanks very much. All the best to you and yours."

When the woman has left he turns back to Stephie. "What else?"

Stephie starts reading again: "Two pounds of oatmeal . . ."

"Let me see," the shopkeeper says, taking the list out of her hands. "Oats, yeast, peas . . . "

He takes things down from the shelves and weighs them for her order. There are no more canned peas on the shelf.

"Sylvia, get me some peas from the storeroom."

Sylvia looks up over the edge of the magazine. "They're on the top shelf. I can't reach."

The shopkeeper sighs. "Well, keep an eye on the candy, then, while I go."

"Sure." Sylvia smiles.

Stephie feels a blush rise. As if she might try to steal their candy!

The shopkeeper returns with the peas. Stephie pays and receives her change.

"May I please see the bookmarks?" she asks.

"Are you buying?"

"Yes."

"They're not on your list. Are you allowed?"

Stephie would really like to take her canvas bag and walk out. But this is the only shop on the island, and she needs presents for Nellie and Uncle Evert.

"I've got money of my own," she answers brusquely.

"Let me see."

Stephie takes her two coins out of her left-hand coat pocket. Sylvia stares in curiosity from behind her magazine.

"And where's the change I just gave you?"

Not until Stephie holds out the coin purse with Aunt Märta's small change does the shopkeeper agree to take down the box of bookmarks. Stephie chooses two sheets: one with angels resting on puffy clouds, the other with girls carrying baskets of flowers. She buys a pack of razor blades for Uncle Evert.

She still has a little money. She's tempted to spend it on candy, but decides to save it instead.

When she leaves the shop she notices it has started to snow. It's getting dark out, too. Aunt Märta's probably annoyed with her for taking so long.

The heavy bag bangs against her leg with every step, and the handle cuts into her palm. She moves the bag from hand to hand and back again on the way home. She even has to stop and rest.

"Is that you, Stephie?" she hears a man's voice shout.

It's Uncle Evert, coming up behind her on the road. He's soon alongside her, and she realizes he's on his way home from the fishing boat.

"That's a big bag for a little girl like you," he says. "I'll take it from here."

Uncle Evert carries the bag as if it were light as a feather.

"Look," he says. "The snow's sticking. I think we're going to have a white Christmas." He extends a large, warm hand, taking hers. "Don't worry," he tells her. "Everything's going to be all right."

twenty-three

On Christmas Eve Stephie eyes Aunt Märta uneasily as she opens the package with the pot holder in it. Will she find it ugly and uneven? No, Aunt Märta seems pleased. She thanks Stephie and hangs it right up on a hook by the stove.

Uncle Evert gives Stephie a paint box and brushes and a pad of watercolor paper. Aunt Märta gives her a cap and mittens she's knitted in a matching pattern. Stephie can't figure out how Aunt Märta managed to knit them without her noticing. The wool smells of mothballs.

Lying in bed later, she hears the voices of Uncle Evert and Aunt Märta from their bedroom.

"You ought to have bought her a few more things," says Uncle Evert. "The kind of trinkets girls like."

"Trinkets," Aunt Märta snorts. "What she needs are warm clothes."

"True enough," says Uncle Evert. "But children need different things for different reasons."

"Are you telling me I don't know what's best for the girl?"

"Not at all."

"So what are we arguing about?"

The conversation ends. A little while later, Stephie hears Uncle Evert's voice again.

"She's a fine girl. I'm glad we took her in."

The wind begins to whine outside Stephie's window and she doesn't hear Aunt Märta's reply.

◊   ◊   ◊

They've been invited to spend Christmas Day at Auntie Alma and Uncle Sigurd's. There are lots of others there, too. Everyone's related, and for the first time Stephie real-izes that Aunt Märta and Auntie Alma are related, too—they're cousins.

Nellie gives Stephie a Christmas present, a tin of can-dies, hard on the outside but with soft chocolate centers. The tin is pretty, with a blue-and-gold pattern.

"You can keep things in it afterward," Nellie points out.

Nellie isn't wearing her coral necklace, as she usually does when she's dressed up. Her soft, pale neck looks very bare without it.

"What was in Sonja's package?" Stephie asks her, trying to sound nonchalant.

"A rubber frog," Nellie says. "It hops when you squeeze a ball."

"Did you give her a present?"

Nellie nods.

"What was it?"

Nellie doesn't answer, just looks away, her bottom lip quivering slightly.

"You didn't give her your coral necklace, did you?"

Nellie nods again.

"Idiot," Stephie says. "What do you think Mamma will say when she finds out?"

"You were the one who told me to!"

"Well, you should have known I didn't mean it."

"What did you say it for, then?"

"I was kidding," Stephie says. "I never thought you'd be dumb enough to give away Mamma's coral necklace."

"I'm going to write and tell her," Nellie says. "I'll tell her you tricked me into it." She looks as if she might burst into tears.

"Oh, it's done now," Stephie hurries to say. "Come on, let's go see what Elsa and John are up to."

◊   ◊   ◊

After Christmas the weather turns colder. The air is raw and damp, full of salty humidity from the ocean. It prickles their cheeks and stings their nostrils. The steep islets Stephie can see from the bay window are capped with snow. They remind her of mountaintops. It's as if the mountains had sunk under the water and left only their tops protruding.

Along the shore and in the inlets, the ocean is frozen over. The ice is a dull gray-green, ribboned with white snow.

140

Farther out, the open water gleams, steel blue. Stephie walks on the beach and feels the thin ice shatter, crunching under her feet. Sometimes she goes right through the layer of ice and snow and down into the stiff, frozen seaweed.

Stephie likes the snow; it transforms the island from gray to white. She makes snowballs and finds targets to aim at, like the rocks out in the water. She slides down the slope behind the house over and over, until Aunt Märta scolds her, saying she'll wear out her boot soles.

By the school there's a real sledding hill. Nellie got a sled for Christmas, and she spends hours and hours at the hill every day with her friends. She'd probably lend it to Stephie if she asked, but Stephie doesn't feel like asking. She hasn't got anyone to go sledding with anyway.

Uncle Evert is out on the fishing boat again. He comes home the morning of New Year's Eve. It's a beautiful day, with a blue sky. The air is clear. Stephie's sitting at the table in her room, using her new paints.

"You ought to be outside on a day like this," Uncle Evert says. "Youngsters need fresh air."

"I was out this morning," Stephie replies.

"The sledding hill over by the school was jammed with kids."

Stephie nods, not looking up from her painting. Uncle Evert sits quietly for a while, just watching her.

After coffee Uncle Evert asks Stephie to come outside with him. She buttons her coat and puts on her new cap and mittens. Uncle Evert holds the door open as if for a fine young lady, and she accompanies him out onto the front steps.

At the bottom of the steps is a sled. It was red once, but the paint is worn and peeling. It's a fine sled, though, made of narrow slats and soft, curved runners.

"Do you like it?" Uncle Evert asks.

"Is it for me?"

Uncle Evert nods. "It's been standing in the shed for years. We'll give it a coat of paint, but I thought maybe you'd like to try it first."

"Whose was it before?" Stephie asks, but Uncle Evert's already ahead of her, pulling the sled toward the slope behind the house.

Stephie sleds for a while. Uncle Evert asks if she'd like to go to the big sledding hill right away, but Stephie wants to paint her sled before she takes it there. They carry the sled down to the basement, and Uncle Evert teaches her how to sand off the old paint. When the surface is smooth he finds a can of paint and a little brush.

It takes a long time to get the brush in between the slats and to do all the edges. When they're finished painting, though, it's as shiny and red as new.

"It'll be dry by morning," Uncle Evert tells her, "and you'll be able to take it out."

In the blue dusk of early evening they roll firm snowballs and put them in a ring to make a snow lantern at the bottom of the front steps. Aunt Märta gives Stephie a little candle to set in the middle. On top of the first ring they make a second, slightly smaller one. Carefully they go on constructing a pyramid of snowballs, until they reach the very top, where there's room for only a single snowball.

Uncle Evert takes out some matches and lights the

candle. It shines from inside the lantern, giving off a lovely glow, a soft, reddish sheen that brightens the whole area.

Stephie sighs. "It's gorgeous."

Aunt Märta comes out onto the steps to admire their handiwork.

"Very pretty indeed," she says.

Coming from Aunt Märta, that's quite a compliment.

To celebrate the coming of the new year, they have their dinner in the front room, saved for special occasions. Aunt Märta's made a roast with potatoes, gravy, and peas. It feels like a real celebration, in spite of the fact that it's just the three of them.

Back in Vienna, the Steiners would have company for dinner on New Year's Eve, another family with two children Stephie and Nellie's ages. They'd set the table for a party, with a white cloth and folded napkins, gold-edged china and silver cutlery. Candles made the wine in the grown-ups' glasses gleam like enchanted gems. The housemaid, in her black dress and white apron, carried in the platters and served each person, while the cook perspired over the pots and pans in the kitchen.

After the meal all four children were sent to rest in the nursery. They would lie there whispering and giggling, much too excited to sleep. Mother came and got them at a quarter to twelve, and they would all go out onto the balcony and listen to the many church bells in Vienna ringing in the new year.

"May I stay up until midnight?" Stephie asks.

"Absolutely not," Aunt Märta replies.

"Oh, why not?" says Uncle Evert. "It's New Year's Eve

only once a year. And a new decade, like tonight, only once every ten years."

Aunt Märta changes her mind. "Well, all right, then," she says. "Put on your nightgown and be all ready for bed. It's just this once, though."

At a few minutes to twelve Aunt Märta turns on the radio. A deep male voice recites a poem:

"Ring out, wild bells . . ."

Uncle Evert opens the window. The ringing of the bells on the radio mixes with the ringing of the island's church bells and with the delicate chiming of Aunt Märta's wall clock.

The year 1939 is over. The new year of 1940 has begun.

"Let this be a better year," Stephie whispers to herself. "Please, please, let it be a better one. I'll try my very best to be good, I promise."

twenty-four

"*Well*, I was certainly taken by surprise," the woman behind the counter at the post office complains. "I never expected such a terrible winter!"

Stephie is waiting her turn. She always tries to pass by the post office on her way home from school to see if there's any mail, hoping for letters from Mamma and Papa.

"That's right," says the woman in the line, taking a bill out of her handbag. "Not even my elderly mother, who's over eighty, remembers a winter as cold as this."

"And with the ocean frozen so far out."

"I've heard you can walk on the ice all the way to Hjuvik now."

Stephie listens alertly. Hjuvik's on the mainland, north of Göteborg. Imagine being able to walk all the way there!

Down at the little harbor, all the boats are frozen in

port. The fishermen have to chop runnels in the ice covering the bay and pull the boats through the ice out into the open water. When Uncle Evert comes back from a fishing trip, his overalls are frozen stiff, like armor.

"Do you think it has something to do with the war, Mrs. Pettersson?" the post office cashier asks.

"Goodness only knows," the lady answers, shaking her head. "These are evil times."

"Evil indeed," the cashier agrees, counting the lady's change onto the counter.

Mrs. Pettersson takes her package, says goodbye, and leaves. At last it's Stephie's turn.

"Hello. Is there any mail for the Janssons?"

"Hello, young lady," the cashier says. "Let me have a look." She sorts through the drawers, then shakes her head.

"Not today."

Stephie bites her lip in disappointment. No letters from home since before Christmas. None to her and none to Nellie.

"Wait a moment," the cashier says. "I'll just check to make sure there's been no mistake." She looks again, but to no avail. "I'm sure you'll hear soon," she says comfortingly. "Come back tomorrow, maybe there'll be a letter then."

"Thank you," says Stephie.

The snow scrunches under her boot soles on the steps outside. Last year's winter boots pinch her toes, but she doesn't dare tell Aunt Märta she needs new ones.

Sylvia and Barbro come toward her, walking in the direction of the shop. Sylvia is wearing a furry white rabbit hat. Barbro has a similar one, but gray. Those hats are in style this winter. Stephie just has her knitted cap with a tassel.

"What are you staring at?" Sylvia asks.

"Nothing."

"No-thing" Sylvia imitates. "Can't you say 'nothing'? You'd better learn Swedish if you're going to live here."

Stephie doesn't answer. She takes a few steps to go by them, but the two girls block her way.

"Let me pass," Stephie says.

"What are you in such a hurry about?" Sylvia asks. "We thought we'd give you a Swedish lesson. Say 'nothing.' "

"Nothing." Stephie does her very best.

"What do you think?" Sylvia asks Barbro. "Does that sound like Swedish to you?"

"Nope," says Barbro.

"You'll have to be punished," Sylvia tells her, gathering up a wad of snow. Stephie backs away, but Barbro's already behind her. Sylvia pushes the snow right into Stephie's face, as if she were washing it.

"Look!" She grins. "What a crybaby!"

Stephie starts wiping the snow from her face. While her hands are over her eyes Barbro drops a handful of snow between her coat collar and her neck. Sylvia is gathering more snow to wash Stephie's face again.

The girls are both bigger and stronger than Stephie. There's no use trying to run away.

At that very moment a snowball comes flying through the air and hits Sylvia smack in the middle of her forehead. Sylvia totters and steps back. Barbro lets go of Stephie from behind, turning around to see who threw it.

147

Svante is on the road, making another snowball.

"Two against one, that's cowardly!" he shouts.

Sylvia shakes the snow off her coat.

"Oh, well, we were done anyway," she says to Barbro. "Let's go."

Stephie brushes snow off her hair and coat. She pokes little bits out from under her collar, and wipes her face with her handkerchief. She turns to Svante.

"Thank you for helping me."

"So you're not mad at me anymore, then?" he asks.

"No," Stephie assures him. "I'm not angry."

She can't help giggling. Svante to the rescue!

"Thank you again," she says. "I'd better be getting home."

The next day there is no mail for her, nor the day after, either. On the third day the woman behind the counter at the post office is waving an envelope when she sees Stephie come in through the door.

"Your letter's arrived!" she shouts proudly, as if it were all thanks to her.

Letter in hand, Stephie dashes home and runs up the steps to her room. She tears the envelope open. As usual, there are two letters inside.

My dearest Stephie, her mother writes. *I've finally received the photographs sent by Mrs. Lindberg. You both look so healthy and fit, and what a cute foster sister and brother Nellie has! Mrs. Lindberg looks like a kind woman, too. I'm so sorry there's no picture of your foster mother. I'd really like to know what she looks like.*

I see you've cut your hair. It makes you look older, unless

148

something else is different, too. I begin to see what you'll look like when you're grown up.

"I see you've cut your hair." As if it didn't matter at all. As if Mamma hardly cared.

Ever since the last letter from her mother, Stephie's been worried about the pictures, afraid her mother would be angry with her for cutting her hair. Now it almost feels worse that Mamma isn't angry at all. Has she stopped caring about Stephie altogether?

"Stephie," Aunt Märta calls from the kitchen, "come help with the ironing!"

Aunt Märta has spread a blanket over the kitchen table, and an old, threadbare sheet on top of it. One of Stephie's jobs is to see to it that there's always a hot iron ready. When the one Aunt Märta is using gets cold, Stephie is supposed to hand her a hot one from the stove top and put the cold one back on the wood-burning stove to heat up. She's also supposed to dampen the laundry by shaking a bottle of water with a sprinkle top, and help fold the ironed clothes.

It takes them all the way to dinner to get through the pile of wrinkly shirts, blouses, dresses, and aprons. Stephie doesn't have a chance to read Papa's letter until after the meal.

Stephie, my big girl! Our hopes of making our way to America are dwindling. I know we are asking a great deal of you, and that you are still a child, but I would be very grateful if you could try to help your mother and me.

Papa is asking her for help! Almost as if she were an adult. Stephie reads on eagerly.

Perhaps Sweden, which is not involved in the war, would

take us in. Please ask your foster parents to help you contact the authorities. Tell them that we are being persecuted here, and that we need to get out. For the moment the Germans are not stopping us from leaving, as long as there is a country that will take us in. Do your best, my dear one, and write and tell us how it is going.

She will show them she can do it. The relief committee will surely arrange for Mamma and Papa to come. She'll talk to Auntie Alma after school and ask her to phone immediately.

The next day she goes right to Auntie Alma's after school. She pretends she's come to play with Nellie, but it turns out Nellie is leaving.

"I'm on the way to Sonja's," Nellie says. "We're going to build a snowman in her yard."

"Oh, well," Auntie Alma says. "You come in anyway, Stephie. I'm sure you're ready for a snack, now that you've come all this way."

She puts milk and sweet rolls on the table.

"We don't see much of you nowadays," she says. "But I suppose you're very busy with school and your friends."

Stephie waits until Nellie has left before she speaks up. Taking a sip of milk, she gathers her courage.

"Auntie Alma," she begins hesitantly, "my father's asked me to try to arrange for him and my mother to get permission to come here. Things are very difficult for them at home now."

Auntie Alma looks distressed. "Oh dear," she says. "I would help you if I could. But politics . . . I can't get involved. Sigurd wouldn't like it."

150

"Politics?" Stephie doesn't see what Auntie Alma means.

"Well, what do we really know about what's going on down there? After all, they wouldn't put innocent people in prison, would they?"

Stephie stares at Auntie Alma's round face and her hair, curling at the temples. She has always thought Auntie Alma seemed kind, but at this very moment she's afraid the kindness is a kind of barrier, one that Stephie can't penetrate.

"Thank you for the snack," she says. "I have to go now."

◊ ◊ ◊

Uncle Evert is out on a long fishing trip and isn't expected back for another week. Aunt Märta is her only alternative.

"I heard from my father," Stephie begins.

Aunt Märta nods without looking up from her darning. "Ah."

"They haven't been granted entry visas to America. Papa doesn't think they will be, either."

"Our destinies are in the hands of the Lord," Aunt Märta replies.

Stephie feels like grabbing her and shaking her up.

"They can't stay in Austria," she says. "They just can't! Don't you see, Aunt Märta?"

"Don't you use that tone of voice with me, young lady," Aunt Märta retorts.

How could she ever have imagined Aunt Märta would help her? No one can. She'll never see her mother and father again.

Her tears overwhelm her so fast she can't get out of the room first. Stephie is sobbing, loud and hard.

"I want to go home!" she wails. "I want to go home!"

"Settle down now," Aunt Märta says. "I'll phone the relief committee tomorrow. Not that I think it will do any good. But it's the duty of a good Christian to help those in need."

Stephie stares at Aunt Märta through her tears. Aunt Märta's face is solemn and determined. She looks like someone who has made up her mind.

"Go wash your face," she tells Stephie. "And I want no more tantrums, do you hear?"

While Stephie rinses her burning-hot cheeks with cold water, she thinks that maybe there is a glimmer of hope. If anyone can make people do what she wants, it's Aunt Märta.

twenty-five

"**What** did they say?"

Stephie's in the kitchen doorway, out of breath and red-faced. She's run the whole way home from school.

Aunt Märta, standing at the stove, turns toward her.

"What on earth is this? Coming in here with your snowy boots on? Go right out in the vestibule and take them off!"

Stephie obeys. By this time she knows Aunt Märta well enough to be sure she will never get an answer to her question until she does.

"Wipe up that mess," Aunt Märta instructs her when she comes back in.

Stephie takes the floor rag and wipes up the few little wet spots she can barely see on the floor. She rinses the rag, wrings it out, and hangs it up to dry.

"Aunt Märta, did you phone the relief committee?"

"I s'pose you think I haven't got anything better to do than spend the whole day on the telephone," Aunt Märta says.

"Not at all," Stephie placates. "I was just wondering . . ."

"It took me over an hour," Aunt Märta tells her.

"I'll peel the potatoes," Stephie offers. She has to improve Aunt Märta's mood to find out what's happening.

"Yes, please," Aunt Märta, says, softening up a little. "Use the enamel basin."

Stephie pours water into the pale yellow basin with its green edge. She goes to the root cellar and gets some potatoes, then takes out the paring knife.

Aunt Märta's cleaning a cod, pulling out musty-smelling purplish innards from the slit belly. Stephie holds her nose and her breath to escape the smell.

"So, Aunt Märta, did you reach someone at the committee office?" she asks tentatively again.

"Finally, yes."

"What did they tell you?"

"The woman said there was nothing they could do."

The knife slips in Stephie's hand, gliding right off the potato she is peeling. Her left index finger stings and there is a drop of blood.

"Aren't you the clumsy one, though?" Aunt Märta asks. "Let me see that finger."

She holds Stephie's finger under the running water, rinsing off the blood. It's only a tiny cut, but the finger throbs and aches.

"Why not?" Stephie asks.

"Why not what? Let me clean this cut."

"No, no—why can't they do anything?"

"Because the relief committee is only allowed to help children. Government policy. No adult refugees are admitted, unless there are special circumstances."

"And aren't there special circumstances for us?" Stephie asks. "Nellie and I are already here."

"You and five hundred other children," Aunt Märta says. "What if every single one of you wanted your parents to be let in?"

"But my father's a doctor. He would be of use. He could work on the island, and the other nearby islands, if someone could just take him around by boat."

Aunt Märta bandages Stephie's finger. "Well, that's what the lady told me. Sorry to say, nothing to do about it. You finish those potatoes, now."

Stephie peels all the potatoes and rinses them in clean water. If only she could make one single person understand!

There's only one way out. She will have to talk with the ladies on the relief committee herself. If she could tell them everything, show them her father's letter and really explain the whole situation, surely they'd understand they had to help Mamma and Papa.

She'll have to go to Göteborg. But how?

"You can walk on the ice all the way to Hjuvik." Wasn't that what the woman in the post office said? Hjuvik's on the mainland. There would be a bus from there to Göteborg.

On Saturday, Stephie says to herself. *When we get out of school early. I'll have to save my lunch sandwiches, or try to make a couple of extra ones without being seen. I'll dress warmly, and take the little compass Uncle Evert taught me to use.*

twenty-six

On Saturday Stephie puts on double stockings and her thickest sweater. She sneaks the compass into her knapsack and tells Aunt Märta she's planning to go sledding after school, so she'll be staying out.

"Be home for dinner," Aunt Märta tells her.

"May I pack an extra sandwich?" Stephie asks. "To have at the sledding hill if I get hungry?"

Aunt Märta says yes. Stephie folds her father's letter into her coat pocket along with the holiday letter with all the good advice from the relief committee. There's an address on the back of the envelope. When she gets to Göteborg she'll find her way there.

In the warm classroom her stockings begin to itch. Stephie squiggles like a worm in her seat, trying to scratch her thigh without anyone noticing.

156

"What's going on? Have you got fleas?" Britta asks. Since Christmas vacation she has forgiven Stephie enough to at least be on speaking terms again.

"It's these stockings," Stephie replies. "They're new."

Britta nods in complicity. She knows very well how itchy new woolen stockings can be.

◇ ◇ ◇

After school Stephie pulls her sled down to the harbor, but she doesn't want to go out onto the ice in plain view. Someone might see her and wonder where she's headed. So she turns left and walks a little distance along the shore, until she is out of sight, behind a pointed headland.

Not until Stephie has stuck the sled under a bush does she realize that she will somehow have to get back to the island, too. Until that moment her plans have been focused entirely on walking to the mainland across the ice and taking the bus to Göteborg. She hopes the coin she has in her pocket will be enough for the bus fare. Once she arrives in Göteborg, she will ask how to get to the address on the envelope.

But what will happen after that? Will she have to walk all the way back out to the island? Or will the relief committee give her the money for a boat ticket? The best thing would be if she could just wait in Göteborg for Mamma and Papa to arrive.

She thinks her parents would be happier in the city than out on the island. Papa could take the boat to collect Nellie, and they could all rent an apartment in Göteborg. It wouldn't have to be a big one, if only they could all be together again.

Stephie tests the ice with one foot. It doesn't crack. She takes a few cautious steps. The snow-covered ice feels just as firm as the ground.

She checks her direction using the compass, as Uncle Evert taught her. Her plan is to walk straight east. Surely that will take her to the mainland.

For a short while she is protected from the wind by the island, but once the shore is far behind her a cold wind sweeps in off the ocean. It's lucky she's warmly dressed.

She turns around to look back. This may be the last time she ever sees the island. It's strange to see the harbor, the docks, and the boathouses from out here, to be walking on what is usually open water.

The wind has swept the ice free of snow. She runs a little way to pick up speed, then slides on the smooth ice.

In front of her she sees a little islet with three houses and a couple of sheds. Margit, who's in her class, lives there. She and her brother row to school every day, except now, when they can walk across the ice.

Stephie hurries past the area where she might be seen from the houses, and passes a point. Out of sight, she sits down on a rock at the shore, opens her knapsack, and removes the sandwiches. She can have one now, but will have to save the other. She has a long way left to go; she doesn't know exactly how far it is to the mainland.

Swallowing the last bite of the sausage sandwich, she rinses it down with a swallow of milk from her bottle. Then she gets up, checks her direction again, and walks on.

When she has put the islet behind her, there is nothing but a huge sheet of open ice ahead, endless whiteness as far as the eye can see. The only things sticking up out of the ice are other occasional rocky islets.

The chill penetrates the soles of her boots, making first her feet and then her legs feel very cold. She ought to have stuffed her boots with straw as she remembered reading about people doing in the Alps. Though there wouldn't have been room for much straw in her already too-tight boots.

Stephie stops to check her direction again. Feeling around in her knapsack for the compass, she can't find it. She takes everything out—her sandwiches and schoolbooks— shaking the sack upside down. The compass just isn't there. She must have forgotten it when she stopped to eat.

She turns around and sees the islet far behind her. Should she go back? That would take at least half an hour, and then another half hour to return to this spot. If she just continues straight ahead, she can probably manage without the compass.

The expanse of ice seems never-ending. Now Stephie is cold through and through, in spite of her heavy sweater and double stockings. She eats the last sandwich as she walks. The milk in her bottle has frozen to a white slush.

The worst part is that it's already getting dark. The dusky air is blue, and her shadow on the ice is eerily long and thin. It looks like she's on stilts.

Night falls quickly. Soon she won't be able to see at all. If she stops where she is, she will freeze to death during the night. The snow creaks, and the ice makes clicking sounds. In the far distance she sees the flashing red light of a lighthouse.

When it is nearly pitch black, she sees the contours of land ahead. She begins to hurry. Exhausted and freezing cold, she steps back onto land. She's standing on a stony beach. To the right there's a dock and a boathouse. . . .

Stephie raises her gaze. Straight ahead she sees a white house with high stone steps. It's a house she recognizes.

She must have walked in a circle instead of straight ahead, turning back out to sea instead of toward the mainland as she thought. She walked right around the island in such a wide arc she couldn't see it until she swung around again and struck land on the west side. The lighthouse she saw must have been the same one she usually sees from the top of the hill.

Her whole long trek was completely in vain. She's back where she started. She hasn't been able to do a thing to help her mother and father, not a single thing.

The kitchen window is bright. When she opens the front door she smells fried pork.

"Stephie," Aunt Märta calls from the kitchen, "is that you?"

Aunt Märta heats up the baked beans for her, scolding her for being late.

"For once you could try to keep track of the time," she says. "Didn't I tell you to be back for dinner?"

"I didn't have any way of knowing what time it was," Stephie replies.

"Were you at the sledding hill all this time?"

Stephie shakes her head. "No, we had a bit of a walk on the ice as well."

"What a thing to do," Aunt Märta says. "I hope you're careful. There are places where the ice is very thin, you know."

twenty-seven

Stephie never tells anyone about her adventure on the ice. It's a secret she intends to keep to herself. She picks up the sled on her way home from Sunday school, and explains to Aunt Märta that she left it at Britta's overnight.

When Uncle Evert comes home Stephie fills him in about her father's letter and what the woman from the relief committee said to Aunt Märta on the phone. To her surprise she hears Aunt Märta say:

"It's not fair. There must be some solution."

Uncle Evert sits thinking for a few minutes. "I could write to our member of parliament," he says. "Maybe he can help."

"Member of parliament? What's that?" Stephie asks.

"Parliament," Uncle Evert explains, "is where our decision makers work. There's a member of parliament from these islands. He's just a regular person you can talk to if you're having a problem."

Uncle Evert asks Stephie some questions about her parents before he drafts the letter. On the envelope he writes the man's name and, on the line below, "Parliament of Sweden." Stephie walks with him to the post office, where he mails it to Stockholm. The woman behind the counter looks impressed.

"So, you're getting involved in politics, are you?" she asks.

"Sure am," Uncle Evert answers.

When they've left the post office, Stephie and Uncle Evert have a good laugh about the curious look the woman gave him.

"She'd give anything to know what's in that letter," Uncle Evert says, chuckling.

Now Stephie waits eagerly not only for letters from her parents but also for an answer from Stockholm. She imagines it arriving in a long, narrow envelope with gold edging and the blue-and-yellow Swedish coat of arms. Inside there will be a letter saying that her parents are welcome to come live in Sweden.

The weeks pass and no answer arrives. The cold weather persists. At school the children keep their coats on. One Saturday in early March Miss Bergström tells the class the school is going to close for a few weeks as there isn't enough fuel to keep the schoolhouse heated.

"We have to economize, what with the war," she tells them. "So we'll have a 'fuel break' until after Easter, when the weather should have warmed up."

She gives them assignments to do at home, arithmetic problems to solve and spelling to work on.

Stephie misses school. The days pass so slowly. She's in suspense, waiting for an answer from Stockholm, for school to start again, for spring to arrive.

◊   ◊   ◊

Easter is early that year. The ocean is still frozen over; the island's still covered with snow. The children and young people devote a lot of time during the week leading up to Easter to gathering wood and other things to burn, and carrying it all up to the highest point on the island, where the Easter bonfire will be.

"You have to be able to see the fire from a long way off," Nellie explains to Stephie as they trudge up to the top of the hill with some scraps of wood. "So everyone will see our bonfire as the biggest one on any of the islands."

The bonfire will be on Easter Eve, after sunset. At midday Stephie makes her usual trip to the post office. On the way, she sees some little old ladies, but they are not dressed in black as the old ladies on the island always are. These ladies are wearing brightly patterned skirts, aprons, and head scarves.

When she gets closer, she sees that they are children. Their long skirts are dragging on the ground. One of them is carrying a broomstick, the other a copper kettle. Their cheeks are rouged and their noses blackened with soot.

Not until she is almost on top of them does Stephie recognize Nellie and Sonja. What on earth are they doing?

"Give a coin to the Easter witches," Sonja says, holding out her kettle.

Stephie's furious. Her little sister, walking around the village begging, dressed in rags! Imagine if Mamma and Papa knew! She tears the flowery kerchief off Nellie's head.

"Are you out of your mind?" she shouts. "Making a laughingstock of us for the whole island to see!"

"Stop it!" Nellie cries, pulling at the scarf. "Careful of that, it's Auntie Alma's."

"Get out of those rags at once!" Stephie roars. "Go home and wash your face! You look like a beggar. What will people think?"

"You're the one who's out of her mind," Nellie shouts back. "You're dumb! We're dressed up as Easter witches. But I don't suppose you know what an Easter witch is. You think everything always has to be just like back home."

"Sonja, Nellie?" other children's voices shout. Three more little girls come running up. They're dressed up, too, like Nellie and Sonja.

"Have you got much?" one asks.

Sonja holds out her kettle for the others to see. She shakes it and the coins rattle.

Stephie looks from one red-and-black-painted child to the next. Easter witches!

"Can I have my headscarf back, please?" Nellie says. "Everybody dresses up as an Easter witch here. Ask anyone at all, and you'll find out."

Stephie passes Nellie the scarf and turns away. When she gets to the post office, it's closed.

◇ ◇ ◇

That evening, just before dark, she, Aunt Märta, and Uncle Evert go up to see the bonfire. The sky is a beautiful, deep blue.

All the islanders have gathered, young and old, boys and girls, men and women alike. Nellie is there with her friends. They're still in their Easter witch getups.

Per-Erik and a few of the other young men are in charge of the fire. They've got a bucket of kerosene to ignite it with.

"When will it be lit?" Stephie asks.

"Soon," Uncle Evert replies. "But our island's not first. We have to wait for the others."

The deep blue sky shifts toward black.

"Now watch," Uncle Evert tells her. "It's time."

Far, far off to the north, a distant flame flares up. And then another, a little closer by, and another on the island nearest them. Per-Erik pours the kerosene over the pile of brushwood and scrap, and then touches a match to it. A huge flame rises. The dry wood crackles and sparks.

"It's catching well," says Uncle Evert with satisfaction. "The boys have done a fine job."

The relay continues on to the farther islands, the ones to the south. The bonfires burn on the highest hill of each island, making a chain of flame.

The fire is so hot, Stephie has to back away. Her face and front feel as if they're being warmed by the summer sun. At her back, though, it still feels like winter.

Uncle Evert puts an arm around her shoulders. "Are you cold?" he asks.

Stephie shakes her head. The fire is roaring. The flames are drawn high up into the now very dark sky.

On all the islands, Stephie thinks. *On all the islands people are standing around bonfires, getting warm. On every island there's someone asking a child if she's cold. On all the islands, people can see the fires from the other islands.*

Stephie likes that thought.

twenty-eight

"*Which* of you will be going on to secondary school next fall?"

Miss Bergström is behind her desk on the first day of school after Easter. The children haven't really settled back in yet. They seem to have forgotten how to sit still during their several weeks' break.

Sylvia and Ingrid raise their hands right away. Three boys raise theirs, too.

"No one else?"

Stephie raises her hand.

"Stephanie?" Miss Bergström asks.

"Yes," she answers. "I want to go on to grammar school, too."

Miss Bergström nods.

"Fine," she says. "Six, that's more than usual. I plan to

give you some extra tutoring for the rest of the semester. You'll be staying an hour longer than the others every day from now on. Here are the titles of two books I want you to get by next week."

She writes the names of two books on the blackboard. Stephie copies them carefully into her exercise book. One is a math book, the other is called *The Tales of Ensign Stål.*

When the school day is over, Miss Bergström asks Stephie to stay behind for a few minutes.

"You're a good pupil," she says. "I'm pleased that you are going to be able to continue your schooling. And there will be German lessons at grammar school, too. You'll like that."

"Yes," says Stephie, wondering what Miss Bergström is really getting at.

"Those books I asked you to get," she goes on, "the ones we'll be working with this spring. Don't worry about them. I have extras you can borrow. I'll bring them tomorrow, and you can cover them at home."

When Stephie leaves school, the schoolyard is empty. The piles of dirty snow even in the darkest corner are melting, and little rivulets have formed in the gravel.

Now that the snow is finally disappearing, all her classmates have got their bikes out again. After school they rush in a flock to the bicycle stands and pedal off.

There's just one bike left. Vera's squatting down beside it, pumping the back tire.

Stephie approaches her cautiously. This is the opportunity she's been waiting for, a chance to talk to Vera alone.

It should be simple just to ask: "Are you heading home? Want to walk together?" But sometimes the simplest things are hardest. So Stephie decides to open the conversation by talking about something else. If she can just strike up a conversation, surely she and Vera can walk out through the gate together, Vera leading her bike, as if it were the most natural thing in the world for the two of them to be walking home side by side.

Stephie walks over to the bike stand. "Aren't you going on to grammar school?"

Vera looks up. "No," she answers. "My mother can't afford it. And I'm not good enough at school, either."

"You could be, though," Stephie replies. "If you wanted to. You could be . . . an actress, for instance. You're such a good mimic."

"Oh, well," Vera says. "I'll be getting married. Maybe to a rich man, one of the summer visitors. I'll live in the city and have a cook and a housemaid."

She stands up and looks in the direction of the gate. Now Stephie notices Sylvia and Barbro, standing on the road with their bikes. They're waiting for somebody. Vera.

"It's different for you," Vera tells her. "You're the grammar school type."

"Hurry up, Vera," Sylvia shouts. "We're leaving!"

"You don't have a bike, do you?" Vera asks.

"No."

Stephie would rather the other children think she isn't allowed to bike than have them find out that she doesn't know how.

"Too bad," Vera says. "We could ride home together if you did. Bye."

170

She mounts her bike and pedals over to Sylvia and Barbro. Stephie watches them disappear down the road.

Stephie doesn't mention grammar school to Aunt Märta that day. The next day Miss Bergström brings her the books. The math book is much more difficult than the one they use in class. It has problems with x and y instead of numbers.

Stephie takes the books home and asks Aunt Märta for paper to cover them with.

"Isn't it late in the semester to be getting new books?" she asks. "And who gave those to you, anyway?"

"Miss Bergström lent them to me," Stephie replies. "They're for the extra tutoring I'll be taking to prepare for grammar school."

"Really! It's no use your thinking about going on," Aunt Märta snaps. "There'll be no grammar school for you."

Stephie just stares at her.

"But I'm going to be a doctor!" she cries. "I have to go to grammar school."

Aunt Märta barks a short little laugh that sounds more like a cough.

"It's about time you became more realistic and dropped those fine-lady thoughts of yours," she says. "Where do you think you are, after all? Do you think we're made of money? We can't afford room and board in town for you; surely you understand that. And what good would it do? We don't even know how long you're going to be here."

"But what will I do, then, after the school year's over?"

"Help me in the house," Aunt Märta tells her. "And

when autumn comes you can take the home economics course here on the island. Like most of the other girls do."

"I don't want to take some old home economics course!" Stephie protests. "I want to stay in school, real school!"

"That's the last I want to hear about it. You're too stubborn for your own good. Now you go up to your room and stay there until you're ready to apologize."

The following day Stephie takes the math book and *Ensign Stål* back to school without paper covers. She asks to speak with Miss Bergström at recess.

"I'm not allowed to go on to grammar school," she tells her.

Miss Bergström frowns. "Hadn't you asked permission before you raised your hand?"

"No."

"I see," Miss Bergström says. "Do you know what? I'm going to come and have a word with the Janssons."

"Oh, thank you," Stephie gasps. "Miss Bergström?"

"Yes?"

"Wait until Friday. Uncle Evert's coming home then."

"Will he be easier to persuade?"

Stephie nods. "I think so. And Miss Bergström? Please don't say anything in class. About me not being allowed to go on."

Miss Bergström understands. "No, I won't."

On the way home Stephie stops in at the post office as usual. There is nothing but a brown envelope with a typed address, to Evert Jansson. Aunt Märta sets it on the sideboard for Uncle Evert's return.

twenty-nine

On Friday there's fried mackerel for dinner, as usual.

"Stephie's teacher is coming over this evening," Aunt Märta says when they are finished eating. "She wants a word with us."

"What kind of trouble are you in now?" Uncle Evert asks Stephie, but she can hear from his tone that he's joking.

"None at all," Stephie replies. She doesn't want to talk about grammar school when Aunt Märta's listening.

"We'll see about that," Aunt Märta says.

After dinner Stephie is instructed to dust the front room, although she dusted it just a couple of days before. Aunt Märta says things have to be spic and span when Miss Bergström comes.

Uncle Evert comes in while she's straightening up.

"Uncle Evert," Stephie begins.

"Yes?"

Just then he catches sight of the brown envelope on the sideboard. He takes out his pocketknife and cuts the seal.

"You know," Stephie goes on, "Miss Bergström's coming over because . . . well, not because of anything I've done wrong."

"Now don't you worry," Uncle Evert tells her distractedly, pulling a typed sheet of stationery out of the envelope.

"I'm not worried," Stephie replies. "But I . . . I'd really like . . . "

She stops talking because she can tell Uncle Evert isn't listening. The more of the letter he reads, the deeper the crease in his forehead becomes.

Stephie lifts a potted plant to dust the windowsill.

"Stephie," Uncle Evert says, "there's something I need to talk to you about."

"What's that?"

"This letter. Remember how I wrote to our member of parliament?"

As if she could have forgotten!

"Well, this is his answer," Uncle Evert continues.

"What does he say?"

Uncle Evert sighs. "He says there's nothing he can do for your mother and father."

The plant slips out of Stephie's hands, crashing to the floor.

"They can go to the Swedish embassy in Vienna and apply for entry permits, but their chances aren't good. He writes that he has investigated the matter and as far as he can determine hardly any adult Jewish refugees are being granted entry to Sweden."

Aunt Märta hurries into the room. "What broke?" she wants to know.

She sees the pot, and the soil and pieces of plant on the floor.

"Good grief, you are the clumsiest thing! My best geranium! And now, of all times."

"Let the girl be," Uncle Evert scolds. "Can't you see she's upset?"

He passes the letter to Aunt Märta. She reads it, then says in a gentler voice, "Would you please get the broom and clean up before Miss Bergström arrives?"

Stephie does as she's told. When she's finished she asks Uncle Evert if she may read the letter herself. She takes it up to her room and tries to decipher the difficult Swedish: *". . . a certain amount of restriction regarding the issuing of visas . . ."*

She hears the front door open downstairs.

"Good to see you, Miss Bergström," Aunt Märta says. "Do come in."

"Thank you," Miss Bergström replies. "Is Stephanie at home?"

"Yes, but—"

"I just want to say hello to her, too," Miss Bergström adds.

"Stephie!" Aunt Märta calls up the stairs.

Stephie sets the letter aside and goes down.

"Good evening, Stephanie," Miss Bergström greets her.

She sounds so formal. Miss Bergström is the only person on the island who calls her Stephanie.

"Good evening, Miss Bergström."

"How fortunate you are to live here," Miss Bergström begins. "You even have a room of your own."

"Yes, it's upstairs."

"Good heavens," Miss Bergström goes on. "I'm sure I haven't been in this house for fifteen years. Not since Anna-Lisa—"

"Please come in," Aunt Märta interrupts. "Come in and sit down."

She shows Miss Bergström into the front room, where she's set the table with coffee cups, a creamer, and a sugar bowl. It's the best china, with gold edging and a flower pattern, not their everyday tableware. On a tall cake plate, there's a sponge cake waiting to be served.

"Stephie, would you bring in the coffee, please?" Aunt Märta says while Miss Bergström is shaking Uncle Evert's hand.

Stephie pours the hot coffee from the stove into the china pot Aunt Märta has taken out. Carefully she carries it in and sets it on the table. It's heavy. Aunt Märta pours.

"Why don't you take a piece of cake up to your room?" she says to Stephie.

So she's not to be allowed to hear the discussion! Stephie looks at Miss Bergström, who just sits silently, stirring her coffee.

Stephie cuts a piece of cake and carries it out on a saucer.

"Please shut the door behind you."

Stephie stands out in the hall for a while, listening to the mumble of voices through the closed door, unable to make out the words. Just as well to go upstairs, then.

She sits on her bed, eating her cake nervously. She gets crumbs on her bed, but doesn't care.

Half an hour later she hears the front room door open.

"But Miss Bergström, you know I'd be very happy to walk you home," she hears Uncle Evert say.

"There's no need at all," Miss Bergström replies. "Do promise me you'll consider the matter."

"We'll think it over," Aunt Märta answers.

"Thank you for the coffee and the delicious cake," Miss Bergström concludes.

"It was nothing. Thank you for coming."

They're out in the hall now.

"Good night, Stephanie," calls Miss Bergström up the stairs.

"Good night."

"See you on Monday."

The front door opens and closes. Miss Bergström's visit is over.

thirty

"*Things* don't always work out as we hope," Uncle Evert tells Stephie. "We have to take life as it comes and make the best of it."

Stephie draws her fingernail across the oilcloth on the table, saying nothing. There's nothing to say. They've made up their minds. She's not going to grammar school come fall.

"Don't sit there moping," says Aunt Märta. "You've nothing to be dissatisfied about. We care for you as if you were our own. You should be grateful."

"I am," says Stephie, her voice breaking.

"Chin up, now," Uncle Evert says. "Everything will be all right, you'll see. If you end up staying here for a long time, we will make sure you learn a useful trade in the end."

"May I please be excused?"

Aunt Märta nods. "All right."

"Thank you for a nice dinner."

Stephie puts on her coat and walks down to the beach.

The spring sun has melted the ice during the last few days, and the snow is melting, too, dripping from the boat-house roof. A black-backed gull is crying overhead. "Caw, caw, caw!" He sounds as if he's laughing at her.

She sits down on the upturned dinghy, gazing out across the water. There are still a few sheets of ice in the inlet. The water glistens, clear blue. Far away, on the other side of the ocean, is America. Will she ever get there?

◊   ◊   ◊

For the second time, Stephie carries the books back to Miss Bergström, who accepts only the math book.

"Please keep this one, anyway," she says, passing *Ensign Stål* back to Stephie once again. "You can read it and return it to me when you're done."

Stephie reads a few of the verses in the book, about a long-ago war. It's not the kind of poetry she likes.

Every day after school when Stephie sees Sylvia, Ingrid, and the three boys who are staying on for extra tutoring, her heart aches. If she had been one of them, wild horses wouldn't have been able to keep her away from school. As things are, she feels some satisfaction when a spring cold forces her to stay home for a few days.

Because Stephie's sick, Aunt Märta lets her sleep as late

as she likes in the morning. One day Aunt Märta has already left for the village when Stephie gets up. Barefoot, she tiptoes downstairs in her long nightgown.

The morning sun slants in through the window of the front room. Stephie turns on the radio, raising the volume so she can hear it in the kitchen. She slices some bread, and then gets the butter cooler and the milk pitcher from the pantry.

Right in the middle of a piece of music, there is an interruption. First silence, then static, then a solemn voice comes on:

"This is a special broadcast from the Swedish news agency. German troops have invaded Norway and Denmark. Norwegian radio reports that the Germans took control of the Norwegian ports at three in the morning. German battleships are now in the Oslo fjord. . . ."

Stephie stands still as a statue in the middle of the kitchen floor, pitcher in one hand, butter cooler in the other.

Oslo's not far away at all. If the Germans have gone to war against Denmark and Norway, Sweden will probably be next.

When Aunt Märta gets back, she finds Stephie sitting on a chair with her feet tucked in under her, still in her nightgown. Her breakfast is on the kitchen table, untouched. The news broadcast has ended but she hasn't turned the radio off. Ordinarily Aunt Märta would have been annoyed and scolded Stephie for listening to music.

"You've heard?" is all she says now.

"Yes."

"I found out at the post office," Aunt Märta says. "It's awful. Just terrible."

They keep the radio on all day. Stephie stays in the front room, wrapped in a blanket. Every time there is a news broadcast, they hear how more and more towns in Norway have fallen to the Germans.

"Owing to the danger of deep-sea mines, Swedish fishermen are warned against going into the straits of the Skagerrak, and possibly also the Kattegatt," a crackling voice announces at noon.

The *Diana* is out on a long fishing trip, somewhere in the Skagerrak. Uncle Evert and the others aren't expected home until the day after tomorrow.

"Uncle Evert . . . ," says Stephie.

"Don't worry," Aunt Märta says brusquely, but Stephie sees that her hands are tense, pale fists.

Just as the reporter is describing the ongoing battle between German and British warships in the North Sea, the telephone rings.

". . . severe storm, seas extremely choppy . . . ," the voice on the radio says.

Stephie and Aunt Märta look at each other. Stephie is sure she and Aunt Märta are having the same thought: What if something has happened to Uncle Evert? Aunt Märta gets up and answers the phone.

"Hello?" She listens for a moment, then passes the receiver to Stephie. "It's for you."

Stephie exhales. "Hello?" she repeats into the black receiver.

At first all she can hear is sniffling. Then Nellie's voice:

181

"Stephie?"

"Yes?"

"I'm so scared. Do you think they'll come here?"

"I don't know. I'm frightened, too."

"Can I come be with you?"

"Just a minute, let me ask."

Aunt Märta doesn't mind if Nellie comes over.

Auntie Alma and the little ones come, too. Auntie Alma seems very upset. She and Aunt Märta speak in hushed tones.

". . . taken in at some port . . ."

". . . maybe by radio . . ."

At five in the afternoon the newscaster reports that the Germans have occupied the main post office and the police station in Oslo, and that German aircraft have landed in southern Norway. Aunt Märta turns the radio off.

"I'm going to make some dinner," she says. "We have to eat, in any case. You're all welcome to spend the night, if you like."

They put Auntie Alma and the little ones up in the guest room, and Nellie is supposed to sleep on a mattress on the floor of Stephie's bedroom. This is the first time in nearly eight months they've shared a room.

"Stephie?" Nellie asks when they've turned out the lights.

"Mmm?"

"Can I sleep in your bed?"

"I've got a cold. You'll catch it."

"I don't care."

Nellie cuddles up in Stephie's bed with her. Her feet are icy cold on Stephie's legs. Stephie puts her arms around her.

"If they come here, what will you and I do?" Nellie asks.

"We'll move somewhere else," Stephie replies.

"Where to?"

"To . . . Portugal."

"Portugal," Nellie says. "It's hot there, isn't it? They don't have snow, do they?"

"Right," Stephie answers. "Only sandy beaches and palm trees as far as the eye can see."

"That was what you said it would be like here, too," Nellie reminds her.

"I remember. I was wrong."

"Will Mamma and Papa also be able to go to Portugal?"

"I don't know," Stephie says. "We'd better go to sleep now."

Nellie stops talking and turns over. Stephie thinks she's fallen asleep, but then she hears her sister's voice again in the darkness.

"Stephie? Just think if the war goes on for so long Mamma and Papa don't recognize us when it's over."

"They'll recognize us," says Stephie. "Even if the war goes on for years. I know they will."

They fall asleep cuddled close together. Like when they were little, in the nursery at home.

thirty-one

Uncle Evert comes home the next evening, earlier than expected. He is pale and exhausted. A fishing vessel from one of the nearby islands was blown up by a mine.

"Six men dead," Uncle Evert tells them. "It could just as easily have been us. We were only a couple of hundred yards away."

His hands tremble slightly as he peels his potatoes. Stephie notices and realizes that Uncle Evert is frightened, too.

"Will you be able to go on fishing?" Aunt Märta asks.

Uncle Evert nods. "We can't stop fishing. We must simply place our destinies in the hands of the Good Lord. And pray for the war to end quickly."

Stephie tries to say something, but her throat has constricted and she can't get the words out. She swallows hard.

"Do you have to fish so far out at sea?" she finally manages to ask. "Can't you stay closer to the coast?"

"We only get the big catches way out. The ocean is full of fish there."

"And of dangers," Aunt Märta adds. "Dangers enough without people making it even riskier. That's a sin."

Stephie looks at Uncle Evert and notices that his eyes have an expression she's never seen before. The same expression her mother had when she looked at Stephie's father after he'd returned from the labor camp. It was when the two of them were sitting talking in the evenings, thinking the children were asleep. Stephie would lie awake, squinting at her parents and straining to hear their whispers, though she never caught more than occasional words.

"When we passed Marstrand we saw warships shooting at each other out by the Pater Noster lighthouse," Uncle Evert is telling Aunt Märta. "It was a terrible sight, and an awful sound."

It's not very far to Marstrand, Stephie knows. The war is close to them now.

Orders are given on the radio for everyone to ready their houses for the blackout. If the Germans attack at night, it is important that they not be able to see, from the air or the sea, where there are people and buildings. Aunt Märta sews blackout curtains out of heavy, dark fabric and hangs them up. At dusk, when they turn on the lights inside, they're supposed to pull the curtains shut. Fortunately, it's spring and the evenings are long and light.

At school they are told that all the children living on islands may have to be evacuated to the mainland. Every child is to have a suitcase packed in case the order comes suddenly. Most of the kids seem to find this exciting. Stephie finds it frightening. She doesn't want to be uprooted again, or to have to make another journey to an unknown place with unfamiliar people.

She packs her suitcase with two sets of clothes, her jewelry, and her photographs. Who knows—if she has to leave she may never come back.

What worries her most is that her parents won't know where she is. No one is given an address in advance. And what if she and Nellie are separated?

But after a couple of weeks the official plans change; there will be no evacuation. They unpack their suitcases again.

Sugar is rationed now, like coffee has been since Easter. No one can just go to the shop and buy as much as he or she pleases, only as much as the ration coupons allow. Aunt Märta collects their coupons from the post office, and keeps an eagle eye on Stephie so that she doesn't sweeten her oatmeal too much.

Stephie's hair is getting longer. It's down to her shoulders already and she can make two short braids. She figures it will be really long again by the time she gets to America.

The wind off the ocean is getting warmer. Uncle Evert makes the dinghy seaworthy for the summer, and takes Stephie out rowing.

"Sit over here now and I'll teach you to row," he tells her. "If you're going to live in the islands, it's a skill you'll need."

She sits in front of Uncle Evert, who kneels behind her, helping her control the heavy oars.

At first Stephie finds it very difficult, and the oars shift uncontrollably in the oarlocks. After a while she begins to master the strokes, but it takes practice for her to get the strength right so that both oars glide through the water evenly. Time after time she is too strong on the right side, and so the boat circles left.

"Why do I have to row backward?" she asks. "It's hard not to be able to see where you're going."

"Try sitting frontward and see how that goes."

Stephie turns around on the bench and pulls the oars the other way, from front to back. It's impossible.

There's hardly any wind. A gray-blue haze merges the water and the sky at the horizon. The surface of the water is smooth, with barely a ripple. Just a gentle coursing back and forth, reminding Stephie of the shiny satin of Mamma's finest ball gown. Dove-blue moiré, her mother used to call it. Stephie turns the word "moiré" over and over in her mouth, finding it as soft and lovely as the fabric itself.

"If I kept rowing west, just kept on and on, would I end up in America?" Stephie asks.

Uncle Evert laughs. "Sure, if you managed to keep on course due west, so you didn't bump into Denmark or Norway, you'd bypass Scotland and only have the whole Atlantic left to cross. You'd have to stock up on provisions if you were going to try. And hope for calm weather, like today."

The oars are blistering Stephie's hands, the soft part

187

between her thumb and her forefinger. But she doesn't complain.

Uncle Evert pulls out a wooden reel and lets a long line run from the stern of the dinghy.

"Rest the oars and come hold the line," he tells her.

Stephie raises the oars over the edge of the boat. Cold water drips on her feet. Carefully she steps over the bench toward the stern. The boat feels tippy. She's afraid it will capsize.

"Don't worry," Uncle Evert says. "This boat doesn't tip easily. At least not from the movements of somebody as light as you."

Stephie gets to hold the line, while Uncle Evert rows with powerful strokes.

"Let's hope the mackerel are biting," he says. "Tell me if you feel the line pull."

Stephie thinks the line's pulling the whole time.

"Now!" she says. "I've got a bite."

Uncle Evert comes over and feels the line, then shakes his head.

"That's just the weight of the sinker. When the fish nibble it feels different."

"Like what?"

"You'll know. Lively, not just a dead weight."

Stephie examines the palms of her hands. They're red and tender. She's almost forgotten the line when, suddenly, there is movement between her fingers.

"Now!" she shouts. "Now they're biting."

Uncle Evert rests the oars, comes over to her, and pulls

the line in. A shimmering fish is struggling on one of the hooks.

Although Stephie has watched Aunt Märta clean mackerel many a time since she came to the island, she's never before realized how beautiful a mackerel is. The smooth skin shimmers in black, gray, and silver. She's strangely excited, her heart beating fast.

"What a beauty," Uncle Evert says. "Surely weighs over a pound. You take it off the hook."

Stephie hesitates. She's never touched a living fish before.

Then she seizes the mackerel with both hands. It's not as yucky a feeling as she'd expected. Cold, but not slimy. Uncle Evert helps her remove the hook from its mouth.

Then he takes his knife and slits an incision alongside one of the gills. Stephie looks away.

"This is another thing you need to learn," he says. "How to gut and clean them."

"Ugh, no," says Stephie. "I'll never do that."

Uncle Evert smiles to himself. "Never say never, that's what I say."

They get three mackerel on the line that evening. Aunt Märta cleans them and fries them for dinner. They do taste quite good, actually.

thirty-two

One bright spring evening, just as Aunt Märta is settling in to listen to the evening prayer on the radio, Stephie's head appears around the corner of the door to the front room.

"I've done the dishes and my homework," she says. "May I go out for a while?"

"I suppose so," Aunt Märta replies. "But be home by dark."

Stephie pulls on a cardigan and ties her shoes. Finally it's warm enough for her to put her too-small boots away and wear lighter shoes.

She goes out onto the steps. The air feels cool and fresh against her cheeks.

Aunt Märta's bicycle is leaning up against the house. It has thick tires and a heavy black frame.

If she could learn to row the dinghy she must be able to master Aunt Märta's bicycle, too.

Stephie grasps the handlebars by their wooden grips and leads the bike out onto the road. She pulls it up the hill, getting sweaty and out of breath.

She stops at the top. The road continues in a long downward incline. Not steep. And quite straight. This must be a good place.

Taking a deep breath, she puts her right foot on one pedal. Then she lifts her left foot, tramping down with her right. She tries to get up on the seat, but it's too high. Standing on one pedal, she rolls unsteadily down the hill, gaining speed. It feels exciting and scary, both at once.

Between two outcrops of rock, the road curves left. Stephie turns the handlebars and loses control. The bike totters, she pushes the brakes and skids in the loose gravel. The bicycle topples and Stephie is thrown into the roadside ditch.

I'm dead, she thinks.

But she's not. One of her arms hurts, though, and so do both her knees.

At the sound of brakes in the gravel she looks up, knowing everyone on the island will hear about this and laugh at her.

"Are you all right?" Vera asks.

"I'm not sure," Stephie answers. "My arm . . . I'm afraid it's broken."

"Let me help you up," Vera says. She dismounts from her bike and pulls Stephie out of the ditch. "Is that your bicycle?" she asks.

"No, it's Aunt Märta's."

Vera stands the bike up and inspects it. "Looks all right," she says. "Maybe a little dent over the front tire. But that might have been there before."

"I don't know," says Stephie.

She's feeling less dizzy now. Her knees are just scraped, but her right arm aches.

"Do you think it's broken?" she asks Vera.

Vera feels it gently through the cardigan. "Can you move it?" she asks. "Like this?"

Stephie tries moving her arm up and down. It hurts, but she can do it.

"I don't think it's broken" is Vera's verdict. "Don't you know how to ride a bike?"

It's no use denying it now.

"I'll help you learn," says Vera. "You can't just roll away, you need to know how to turn and to put on the brakes first. Want me to show you?"

"Please."

"Tomorrow," Vera tells her. "After school. It's Saturday, so we won't have homework. I've got to get home now, and you need to wash up and change your clothes."

Stephie glances down at her muddy dress.

"I'll have to come home for the bicycle after school," she says. "Where do you want to meet?"

"Right here?"

"Fine."

"See you," says Vera, hopping onto her bike and riding off.

Stephie walks Aunt Märta's bike the whole way home.

192

It feels like it's growing heavier and heavier. Going down the steep hill to the house demands all her strength; she has to hold back to keep the bike from taking off on its own and pulling her with it.

She leans the bike up against the house and goes in.

"I'm back," she calls, scurrying up the stairs so Aunt Märta won't catch sight of her muddy dress. At the washstand she does her best to rinse the mud off herself and her dress and to clean her scraped knees.

"I see you're learning to ride the bike," Aunt Märta says when she comes back down.

Stephie had been hoping Aunt Märta wouldn't have noticed the absence of her bicycle. But it's eight o'clock and evening prayers were over long ago. Aunt Märta probably went out into the yard and saw that the bike was gone.

"I'm sorry," says Stephie. "I should have asked before I borrowed it."

"That's all right," Aunt Märta answers. "Just take good care of it. And yourself," she adds, glancing at Stephie's scraped knees and stiff arm.

"May I borrow it tomorrow after school?"

"Certainly."

"Thank you."

◊　◊　◊

The next day Stephie hurries home from school. She leads the bike back up the hill again, and down to the meeting place. Vera's already there.

"Come on," she says, taking Stephie to a little side road.

"This is a better spot. You have to practice on flat ground first. We'd better start by lowering the seat."

Vera's brought a wrench, and she loosens the bolt that holds the seat in place, twisting the seat gently downward and then tightening the bolt again.

"Give it a try," she says.

Stephie tries to mount the bike as she did yesterday, but she can't seem to make it balance.

"You have to start pedaling right away," Vera instructs. "I'll hold you from behind. Try again."

Vera holds the carrier in a firm grip. Stephie swings up into the seat and starts to pedal.

"Not so fast," Vera pants as Stephie picks up speed. "Now put on the brakes, but gently."

Stephie backpedals and feels the bike slow down. She puts one foot on the ground.

"Again," Vera tells her. "Steer, and apply the brakes softly when you start going too fast."

Stephie picks up speed again. Vera runs behind the bicycle with one hand on the carrier. Suddenly, though, Stephie stops hearing her footsteps. There's only the crunch of the tires on the gravel. The pedals keep going around, the bicycle follows the curves in the road easily. She's riding all on her own!

A rock in the middle of the road is her downfall. But she manages to put one foot down so that she doesn't crash; she isn't hurt.

Vera comes biking up from behind.

"You're doing fine," she laughs. "You'll be able to bike to school by Monday."

Stephie bikes back and forth along the road all afternoon. Vera helps her get started at first, but after a while she can get her own balance, and Vera bikes alongside her. Their hair and skirts flutter in the spring wind. The salty sting of the sea blends with the scent of earth warmed by the sun. Light green grass is sprouting up alongside the road and between the outcrops of rock.

When they get tired of riding, Vera teaches Stephie how to pump the tires. They crouch down next to each other, hands and arms touching. The wind blows wisps of Vera's hair so it brushes Stephie's cheek.

There are so many things Stephie would like to ask Vera. Why she's always clowning around in class and pretending to be dumber than she is. Why she's friends with Sylvia and her crowd. Whether the two of them, Stephie and Vera, could be friends for real.

But she doesn't ask anything at all. Vera gets up.

"I've got to get home," she says, "and help my mother with the washing."

They bicycle side by side out to the main road.

"Will you be able to bike home now?" Vera asks.

"I think so."

Stephie mounts the bike. She manages to pedal all the way up to the top of the hill, but she leads the bike on the steep downhill, just to be on the safe side.

thirty-three

Stephie spends all Sunday afternoon practicing, up and down hills, and riding the road in both directions. Aunt Märta, who is otherwise quite strict about keeping the Sabbath on Sunday, and who always wants Stephie to do something quiet after Sunday school, agrees immediately when Stephie asks to borrow her bicycle again.

On Monday Stephie bikes to school. Having struggled up the steep hill from the white house, she has a steady decline for the next half mile, and the wind at her back. She doesn't even need to pedal, the bike just rolls on its own. The wind brushes her face gently and the air is full of new smells.

On her way to school, she imagines arriving at the schoolyard, gently applying the brakes at the gate and then leading the bicycle over to the stand, with Sylvia, Barbro, and all the others gaping in astonishment. She plans to act as if there's nothing unusual about her having biked to school. If they continue to stare she'll ask, "What are you staring at? Haven't you ever seen a bike before?"

Then she'll look right at Vera and they'll smile conspiratorially. Vera won't give her away. She's promised.

Intentionally, Stephie takes the last stretch slowly. She wants everyone to be there when she arrives.

As soon as she has put on the brakes at the gate and set one foot on the ground, she begins to look around for her classmates. They're huddled between the bike stand and the outhouse. Sylvia, Barbro, Gunvor, and Majbritt.

And Vera. She's at the center of the crowd. Apparently she's doing one of her imitations. The others are watching her and laughing.

Stephie walks the bike over to the stand. No one notices. She glances furtively toward the group surrounding Vera.

Vera's holding one of her arms as if it's hurt. "Ow, ow!" she cries. "My arm! I think it's broken!"

At that very moment, Gunvor catches sight of Stephie. "Here she comes!" she shouts.

Stephie feels a lump forming in her throat. At first it's ice cold, then it feels hot. It grows larger and larger.

Everybody's staring at her.

"Well, look at her," Sylvia says in her most affected voice, like an adult talking to a child. "The old lady let the little girl borrow her bicycle. Be careful you don't end up in the ditch. Next time there might not be anybody around to rescue you."

Stephie forces herself to ignore them, looking straight ahead as she walks toward the bike stand. She has heard and seen enough: the mocking mouths, the scornful gazes. And Vera's pale, embarrassed face, framed by her fluffy red hair.

On the stairs up to the classroom, Vera catches up with her. "Stephie," she pants. "I apologize. I didn't mean to—"

The lump in Stephie's throat bursts. "Leave me alone!" she exclaims. "You're just like all the rest. I despise you!"

In the fraction of a second before Vera turns away and continues on up the stairs, Stephie sees something in her eyes and recognizes it. She can't pinpoint exactly what it is, but it makes her feel like bursting into tears.

After school Stephie delays leaving the hallway. She doesn't want to arrive at the bike stand at the same time as all the others just to hear more taunting remarks.

When she finally leaves the building, she finds herself hoping to see Vera's mane of red hair somewhere in the schoolyard, hoping Vera waited for her all the same.

But no one is there. Only six bikes remain in the stand. Aunt Märta's looks very old-fashioned and awkward next to Sylvia's blue one and Ingrid's green one.

Stephie rolls the bicycle back out of the stand. Something doesn't seem right. She feels the tires. They're almost flat. The valve caps are off.

They must have done it at recess, since all the air has had time to leak out. It was probably Barbro. Or Gunvor. Or Majbritt. Or even Sylvia, though probably not. She's always cautious about doing anything she might get caught and punished for. Sylvia gives the orders, the others obey.

Stephie searches the ground for the valve caps. She sees something gleaming. A little tack.

Pfff, says the air as it exits from Sylvia's tire. Stephie presses the nail even farther in, until the head is visible only as a shiny little dot. It would be difficult to see it if you didn't know it was there. It's pressed all the way in, as if Sylvia had happened to bike over it on her way to school.

Stephie finds both valve caps, and luckily Aunt Märta keeps a bike pump attached to the frame. Stephie pumps up the tires and rides home.

The next morning they are at the bike stand, waiting for her. When Stephie parks her bike they close in around her. She's their prisoner.

Sylvia is holding something between her thumb and forefinger, so close to Stephie's face she can barely see it. A shiny object.

The tack.

"It was you," Sylvia says. "Admit that you did it!"

Should she deny it? Sylvia would never be able to prove it.

"Confess!" Sylvia says. She's so close, Stephie can feel the heat of her breath.

"Yes, I did it. But you let the air out of my tires first."

"I did not," Sylvia says. "And anyway, that's different. You must apologize now."

"Never."

"Grab her," Sylvia orders.

Barbro grasps Stephie's right arm, twisting it up behind her back. It hurts.

"Did you say 'never'?"

"That's what I said."

Barbro grabs Stephie's hair, pulling her head backward.

"Is that what you said?"

"Right."

Sylvia bends down and grabs a fistful of gravel from the ground.

"Remember when I washed your face with snow last winter? I'll do it again. But with gravel this time."

Stephie looks at Sylvia. She means business. Stephie's only hope is for the bell to ring.

Sylvia takes another step toward her.

"Sorry," Stephie says.

"On your knees."

"No."

"Otherwise it doesn't count," says Sylvia as Barbro presses Stephie to the ground. She falls to her knees in the gravel.

"Say it."

"Sorry."

"Say: 'Forgive me for ruining your bike.' "

"Forgive me for ruining your bike."

"And kiss my shoe."

Sylvia extends her dusty sandal; it's just a few inches from Stephie's face.

"Kiss it!"

Barbro presses hard on Stephie's neck. Stephie presses her lips tightly together before her face touches Sylvia's shoe.

At last the bell rings.

thirty-four

The lawns in front of the little houses in the village are bright green. The low apple trees are covered with pink and white blossoms, and the lilac bushes with clusters of white and purple buds.

The house at the end of the world doesn't have a yard with apple trees and lilac bushes. It's too exposed to the wind off the water. But on the beach little flowers are pushing their way up between the rocks: yellow, white, and every possible shade of pink, from very, very pale to bright rose. In the crevices among the rocks there are patches of wild violets.

A mottled mother duck and her ducklings are on their way to the water. The ducklings are yellow-brown and fluffy. They follow their mother, swimming behind her in an orderly line.

"Come in for a fitting," Aunt Märta calls from inside. She's making Stephie a dress for the last day of school. The fabric is very pretty, white with little pink and blue flowers. Stephie would have liked buttons down the front, a collar and a chest panel. That would look more grown-up, but Aunt Märta says it's too hard for her. So the front is just an ordinary straight bodice. There's a little round collar, and a zipper in back.

"Ow!" Stephie complains when Aunt Märta accidentally pokes her in the shoulder while inserting a pin.

"If you'd just stand still, it wouldn't happen," Aunt Märta tells her. "Vanity is a sin."

But she looks quite pleased with her handiwork, pulling a loose thread off the skirt.

The evening before the last day of school, Aunt Märta irons the new dress and starches a petticoat for underneath it. The fabric feels stiff, rustling when Stephie pulls it over her head.

Stephie is solemn. The dress is her first new piece of clothing since arriving on the island, except for underwear and stockings, which Aunt Märta buys by mail order, and the cap and mittens she gave Stephie for Christmas.

Mounting the bike, Stephie's careful not to wrinkle her skirt. She spreads it out across the carrier, smoothing it with one hand, making sure the fabric won't get caught in the spokes.

The classes gather at school and they walk in single file to the church. Almost all the girls have new dresses. Sylvia's buttons down the front, as Stephie would have liked hers to. But no one has such a full skirt as Stephie.

The head teacher's speech to all the children in the church seems endless. He talks forever about the "dark shadow of war across Europe," encouraging the children to spend their summer not just having fun but also being extra-obedient because of "these terrible times."

The wooden pews are hard, and Stephie's starched petticoat is itchy around her waist.

"Most of you will be coming back to school next autumn," the head teacher goes on. "But the pupils in the sixth grade are having their very last day of school here today. I would like to wish each and every one of you the best of luck, both those of you who are going on to grammar school in Göteborg and those who are leaving school now. Remember, no matter where you find yourselves later in life, you have a mission: whatever you do, do it well."

But what you do and where you are are important, too, Stephie thinks. *I can do the things I want to do well, but not the things I dislike doing.*

"Miss Bergström and I are, of course, especially pleased that so many pupils, five of you, will continue on to grammar school," the head teacher says. "You are a credit to our elementary school."

Sylvia, sitting diagonally in front of Stephie, smiles with self-satisfaction, as if the head teacher were speaking to her and her alone.

"And now," he says, "I will present the achievement awards to the sixth graders. Miss Bergström, would you come forward and assist me, please?"

Stephie's teacher stands next to the head teacher, a little stack of books in her arms. She passes him a slip of paper.

"Ingrid Andersson," he reads.

Ingrid walks to the front, is given a book, shakes the head teacher's hand, and curtseys before returning to her seat.

"Bertil Eriksson."

Stephie turns toward the side aisle and looks at a painting on the wall. It depicts an old man dressed in black, with a stiff, white collar standing straight up and encircling his face like a flower. She wonders if that collar is as stiff and itchy as her petticoat.

Britta nudges her. "Aren't you listening?" she hisses. "That was you."

"Stephanie Steiner," the head teacher repeats. "Isn't Stephanie Steiner here today?"

Stephie stands up, bewildered. "Here," she says.

Miss Bergström smiles. "There you are. Come forward, please, Stephanie," she says.

Stephie squeezes through the row and into the center aisle, walking up to the head teacher and Miss Bergström.

"May I say a few words?" Miss Bergström asks the head teacher.

"Of course."

"It is always a pleasure to reward good students," Miss Bergström begins. "But there is particular satisfaction in presenting an award to a pupil who is so gifted that she is now at the top of the class in spite of the fact that she didn't speak a word of Swedish a year ago. I wish you the very best of luck, Stephanie."

The book they hand her is a thick one, with a beautiful cover. The gold lettering on the cover reads: *Nils Holgersson's*

Wonderful Journey Through Sweden. On the flyleaf Miss Bergström has written, in her elegant script:

> *To Stephanie Steiner, 7 June 1940*
> *May this book aid you in becoming even better acquainted with your new homeland and its language.*
> *From your teacher,*
> *Agnes Bergström*

Back in the pew, Stephie leafs through the book, fascinated by the illustrations. When the organ music begins, Britta has to elbow her in the side again to stand up.

"The summer flowers are blooming . . . ," they sing. Stephie finds it a lovely song, although she doesn't understand the whole text. She's happy about the book, and about what Miss Bergström said. And yet she's feeling sad. Ordinarily she would have been glad summer vacation was beginning. But a summer vacation that doesn't end with going back to school isn't a real summer vacation.

When fall comes, she'll be taking home economics two days a week. "Learning to run a household," as Aunt Märta puts it. But there's so much else to learn in the world!

After the ceremony they return to their classrooms, and their teachers pass out the grades. "Final Grades," it says at the top of the card. Her name, the date, and the grades are written in blue ink.

Mathematics and geometry: passed with great distinction. She has top marks in art as well. All her grades are good except for Swedish, where she gets only a "pass." But in the margin Miss Bergström has written: *Stephanie's native tongue is not Swedish. In consideration of that fact, she has made excellent progress during the school year.*

Biking home, Stephie smells lilacs as she passes the yards. The apple trees have almost finished blooming. White blossoms now cover the ground around the trunks like huge snowflakes.

◇　◇　◇

"Take off your best dress" is the first thing Aunt Märta says when Stephie comes through the door. "We've got to get things ready for the summer guests today."

"Here are my grades," Stephie tells her.

Aunt Märta glances at the report card. "Well done," she says, handing it back.

"I got a book, too. An achievement award."

"You don't say," Aunt Märta answers. Her voice sounds a bit wobbly.

Stephie goes up to her room and changes to an everyday dress. They clean the entire house, every nook and cranny, just as thoroughly as at Christmastime. Tomorrow the summer guests arrive.

Stephie, Aunt Märta, and Uncle Evert will be moving down into the basement, which has one room and a simple kitchen. Stephie is going to sleep on a trundle bed in the kitchen.

Almost everybody on the island rents out to summer guests. Some people just rent out a room, but most turn their entire house over to the summer tenants and live in their basement. Sylvia's family has a second house that stands empty all winter and is rented out just for the summer. So they go on living above the shop, as usual.

Stephie empties her dresser drawers and carries all her things down to the basement. There's a chest of drawers for her in the boiler room, since there's no space in the little kitchen.

She puts her photographs, jewelry box, and diary into an empty shoebox and stores it under the trundle bed. She leaves the painting of Jesus on the wall for the summer guests.

thirty-five

Their summer guests come in a taxi from the harbor the next day. The trunk of the taxi is loaded down with suitcases and boxes.

There are six people in all: an older couple, their two adult children, the daughter's fiancé, and their housekeeper. Stephie hears Aunt Märta call the man "Doctor." Like Stephie's father. He has gray hair and glasses, and looks tired.

His wife is tall and graceful. She was clearly a beautiful young woman once. The daughter is nice-looking, with curly blond hair. She and her fiancé are always holding hands. The son is tall, with contemplative gray eyes and brown hair that hangs down over his forehead.

The best thing is that they have a dog, a brown-and-white fox terrier that jumps right up on Stephie and licks her hand.

"Putte likes you," the doctor's daughter says.

"I hope you aren't afraid of dogs?" the doctor's wife asks.

"Oh, no," says Stephie, patting Putte on the head. "I love dogs."

"You may walk him," the doctor's wife tells her, "whenever you like."

Stephie helps the summer guests carry in their belongings. The son will have her bedroom. She hears his mother call him, and learns that his name is Sven. She wonders how old he is. Seventeen, maybe eighteen.

When everything is in order, the doctor's wife gives Stephie a coin.

"Thank you for helping," she says.

Stephie blushes. "You don't need to pay me."

"Oh, please don't be offended," says the doctor's wife. "Buy yourself some sweets. Incidentally, where do you come from?"

"From Vienna," Stephie tells her, putting the coin in her dress pocket. "Thank you very much."

◊   ◊   ◊

That afternoon Stephie goes to Auntie Alma's. Their summer guests won't be arriving until the next day. Auntie Alma, Nellie, Elsa, and John are just moving the last of their things down to the basement.

"I heard you got a book as an award at school," Auntie Alma says.

"Yes, I did."

"Well, I want you to know how proud Nellie was of her

big sister when she came home and told us. You're certainly a clever girl, I must say."

"Not that it will matter," Stephie answers.

"What do you mean?"

"Being clever at school. Since I'm not to be allowed to continue anyway."

"To grammar school?"

Stephie nods.

"Well, you have to understand Märta and Evert's situation," Auntie Alma tells her. "It's very expensive to have a child who boards in Göteborg. Not to mention the books and all the other costs."

"I think Uncle Evert would let me go. Aunt Märta's the one who's against it."

Auntie Alma sits quietly for a few minutes.

"Has it ever occurred to you that Märta might not want to see you go off to Göteborg?" she asks. "That she would miss you?"

It's so ridiculous Stephie has to laugh. Aunt Märta, miss her!

"She doesn't even like me," she answers. "I can't imagine why she took me in."

"Has Märta ever told you about Anna-Lisa?" Auntie Alma asks. "Or has Evert, for that matter?"

"No. Who's Anna-Lisa?"

"Anna-Lisa was Märta and Evert's daughter," Auntie Alma tells her. "Their only child."

"I didn't know they had children."

"It's fourteen years now since she passed away," says Auntie Alma. "She was twelve when she died."

"What did she die of?"

"Anna-Lisa was never a healthy child. Even as a baby she was often ill. Märta took wonderful care of her and was always very protective. But when Anna-Lisa was eleven she was diagnosed with tuberculosis. She lived her last six months at a sanatorium on the mainland, far away. The doctors said the dry inland country air would do her good. But it didn't help."

"The knitted cap," Stephie says. "And the sled."

"What about them?" asks Auntie Alma.

"Presents I've been given. They must have been hers. Anna-Lisa's."

It's strange to think that the cap and mittens she wore all winter once belonged to another girl, a girl who died before she herself was born. Did Anna-Lisa ever wear them? Or did she die before Aunt Märta finished knitting them?

"Why didn't anyone tell me?" Stephie asks. "Why don't they have any photographs of her at home?"

"It was terribly painful for Märta," Auntie Alma tells her. "She couldn't even bear to see a picture of her afterward. For over a year, Märta walked around more dead than alive herself. If she hadn't had her faith in God, who knows where it would have ended. You should have seen her before, when Anna-Lisa was alive. So different from the way she is now. Full of life and afraid of nothing. She had an answer to every question and never hesitated to speak her mind. Though there was never a harsh word to Anna-Lisa, I'm sure. Märta was as careful of her as if she had been made of china."

"But why did she take me in?"

"I don't know. I've wondered myself. Perhaps out of the desire to save a child, because she wasn't able to save Anna-Lisa."

"Why couldn't I live with you?" The words slip out of Stephie's mouth before she can stop them. "We were supposed to stay with the same family. They promised."

"I know," said Auntie Alma. "I would have been happy to take you both, but Sigurd was against it. He felt one was enough. So the relief committee asked if I could find another family on the island, so you'd at least be close to each other. Märta never hesitated. But she didn't want a little child, and so it was you."

"Stephie!" Nellie shouts from behind the house. "Stephie, come see what we found!"

Auntie Alma smiles. "Run along and play," she says. "It's no use brooding. We have to make the best of our lot in life."

Stephie goes around to the backyard. Nellie and the little ones have pulled up a fat worm in Auntie Alma's potato patch. It's suspended between Nellie's thumb and index finger.

"Just look at this yucky thing," Nellie shouts gleefully.

Stephie takes the worm from Nellie. It squirms between her fingers.

"Let's put it back now," she says. "It wants to be in the soil."

Carefully, she places the worm next to a potato plant. It vanishes quickly down into the ground.

"The worm went home," says John. "To his house."

When Stephie is ready to leave, Auntie Alma calls her inside.

"I've got something for you," she says secretively.

On the kitchen table is a flat, soft package.

"For me?"

"Yes, for you."

"But why? My birthday's not until July."

"I know, but it's something you need now. Aren't you going to open it?"

Stephie removes the ribbon and unwraps her present. It's a bathing suit. Red with white polka dots and a frilly neckline.

"It's beautiful!" Stephie gushes. She holds the bathing suit up to her front. It looks just right.

"I think it should fit you," Auntie Alma says. She smiles. "So now you can swim a lot this summer and not have to spend your time sitting on the beach."

"Do you think," Stephie asks her, "that if Anna-Lisa had lived she would have had to wear some old, hand-me-down bathing suit?"

"If Anna-Lisa had lived," Auntie Alma replies, "you might not have been here at all." She smiles again. "You know, I'd really like to see you try the bathing suit on before you go home."

Stephie goes up to Nellie's room and pulls the bathing suit on. It's perfect. Tomorrow she's going to the beach.

thirty-six

There's a separate door to the basement at the back of the house. Every morning Stephie goes out through it, around the house, and up the front steps. She knocks on the door and waits.

Sometimes the doctor's wife answers, but more often it's the daughter, Karin. The moment the door opens Putte comes running, wagging his tail and licking Stephie's hands and knees. Karin goes and gets his leash from its hook in the hall and clips it onto his collar.

"Do you need any errands run?" Stephie always asks.

Some days there's a letter to mail or something the doctor's wife has forgotten to order from the shop. The shopkeeper hires a messenger boy for the summer, and the boy delivers orders to the summer guests on a bicycle with a big metal box on the front. The summer guests phone in their orders.

If she's going to do an errand at the post office or the shop, Stephie usually takes the bike, tying Putte's leash to the handlebars. He runs alongside. Otherwise she takes him for a walk along little paths too narrow to bike on. Putte noses around, sniffing, straining eagerly at the leash. Stephie almost has to run to keep up.

She's not allowed to take off Putte's leash, but sometimes she can't resist. He just loves to fetch sticks she throws, and always comes when she calls. If Stephie's sitting on a rock, he often comes over and puts his head in her lap, wanting to be scratched behind the ears and under the chin.

When Stephie returns with Putte, she usually finds the doctor's wife and Karin and her fiancé enjoying their morning coffee at the table in the yard. Uncle Evert set up the furniture in the shade over by the rock face. The doctor works in Göteborg all week, and joins his family only on weekends. Stephie doesn't know where Sven spends his time. She imagines him sleeping late.

◊ ◊ ◊

One morning when she's out walking Putte up among the rocks and the scraggly vegetation, she bumps into Sven. She's standing on a boulder gazing out across the ocean. Luckily, Putte's on his leash. She's afraid if anyone in the doctor's family were to see that she sometimes lets him run freely, she wouldn't be allowed to walk him anymore.

215

"Hi there!" Sven calls out. "What a beautiful morning!"

To Stephie there is nothing special about this particular morning. The sun is shining and there is a gentle wind blowing off the water.

Putte recognizes Sven and grows eager. Sven hops down off his rock and approaches them. Putte romps between his legs, begging to be patted.

"Hiya, Putte. Hi, you old thing."

Sven plays with Putte, but not gently, as Stephie does. He's rougher.

"You can let him off the leash now," says Sven. "He won't run away."

He never runs away from me, Stephie thinks, but she doesn't say it.

Sven stops playing with Putte and sits down on a rocky ledge, his feet blocking the path in front of Stephie. She picks up the end of Putte's leash, but stays where she is.

"The ocean," says Sven. "I can look at it forever, can't you? It's always changing."

"Uh-huh," Stephie replies. "Depending on the weather." She wishes Sven would move his feet so she could pass.

"Don't you like the ocean?"

"It's so big. I'd like it better if I weren't on an island. If it was all one."

"One what?"

"One whole place. The people. The city."

"How long have you been here?" Sven asks.

"Since last August. Ten months."

"And your family?"

216

"Mother and Father are still in Vienna. My little sister is here, living with a different family."

"And what are they like, your family here? The Janssons."

"Good," Stephie tells him.

"You're different from them," Sven says. "That doesn't mean you have to be alone."

Putte whines, pulling at the leash.

"I've got to get going," Stephie says.

"Wait," Sven answers. "I'd like to read you something."

He pulls off the little knapsack he's carrying and opens it, rummaging around. He has to retrieve a crumply bag of sandwiches, a thermos, and a sweater before he gets to the thick book at the bottom.

"It's in English," Sven tells her. "Do you speak English?"

"No."

"That's all right. I'll translate." He leafs through the book until he finds what he is looking for. " 'No man is an island, entire of itself; every man is a piece of the continent, a part of the main. . . . ' "

Stephie stands stock-still, absorbed. Sven's voice is different when he reads than when he talks, deeper and calmer.

" 'Any man's death diminishes me, because I am involved in mankind; and therefore never send to know for whom the bell tolls; it tolls for thee.' "

Sven stops and looks up from the page. He and Stephie are both quiet for a few moments. Then Sven closes the book.

"That was all," he says. "But maybe you're too young to understand."

"I understand," Stephie retorts. "Who wrote that book?"

"An American named Hemingway," says Sven. "But what I read you is a quotation from the work of a poet named John Donne, who lived in seventeenth-century England. When you get a little older and have studied English, you'll be able to read the whole thing."

"I'm not going to study English," Stephie tells him.

"Why not? You're good at languages, I can tell from your Swedish."

"I'm done with regular school," Stephie says. "I'm just going to take a home economics course next fall. They can't afford to send me to grammar school."

"That's really too bad," says Sven. "You ought to continue your studies. You've got a good head on your shoulders and should read, think, and write."

He puts his book and other things back into his knapsack.

"If you'd like, I'll lend you some books," he says. "I've got some with me, and I can ask Father to bring more when he comes out from the city. Some German books, too, if you'd like."

"Oh, please, that would be wonderful," says Stephie.

"Feel free to come up anytime. Anyway, aren't I staying in your bedroom?"

"That's right."

"What about that painting?" asks Sven. "Did you pick it out yourself?"

"No," Stephie says emphatically.

"I've turned it toward the wall," Sven tells her. "Don't let Mrs. Jansson know, though. If you'd like I can accidentally knock it to the floor so it breaks."

Stephie laughs. "You don't need to do that," she tells him. Sven gets serious again.

"One night when the room was too hot, I opened the vent, but it turned out to be blocked with a crumpled sheet of paper. A letter. Yours, I assume, since it was in German."

That letter she wrote her first evening on the island, to Mamma and Papa. *If you don't come and get me, I think I'm going to die.* Stephie blushes.

"I didn't read it," says Sven. "Word of honor. Do you want it back?"

"No," Stephie says. "Throw it out, or burn it. But don't let anybody read it. I'm going now. Putte's impatient."

When she is at a distance, Sven shouts, "What's your name again?"

"Stephanie."

She doesn't really know why she didn't just say "Stephie." Maybe because "Stephanie" sounds more grown-up.

"Pretty name," Sven shouts back. "Bye, Stephanie."

Later the same day Stephie goes to the beach with Nellie. She tries to give her a ride on the back of Aunt Märta's bike, but it's hard. Wobbly, and heavy on the uphills.

Nellie's playmate Sonja is at the beach. The three of them lie on their towels, sunbathing on the sand. The water's still cold, but after a while in the sun it's refreshing.

Way out on the far cliffs Stephie sees Sylvia and Barbro with two boys she doesn't recognize. They must be summer guests.

thirty-seven

One day, toward the end of June, Stephie bikes to the shop to buy a package of cookies for the doctor's wife. Putte runs alongside the bike as usual.

Some kids are sitting on the stone wall that encloses the shopkeeper's yard. Sylvia and Barbro are in the middle, each with a summer guest next to her. One is so blond his short hair looks almost white. The other is darker, and freckle-faced.

Vera's there, too. She's sitting at a distance from the others, braiding a chain of dandelions.

Stephie parks the bike and ties Putte to a hook in the wall. Sylvia and Barbro are whispering and giggling with the boys. She can feel their gazes burning on her back as she opens the shop door and goes inside.

When she is paying for the cookies, she hears barking.

"Is your dog making that racket?" the shopkeeper asks grumpily.

"He's not mine, but I walk him."

"Well, you'd better quiet him down."

Stephie puts the package of cookies in her pocket and goes out onto the steps.

Sylvia, Barbro, and the two boys are standing in a ring around Putte, just far enough away that he doesn't have a chance of reaching them no matter how hard he strains at the leash. Vera's still sitting on the stone wall.

Stephie approaches them. Now she sees that one of the boys, the blond one, is holding something. It's a sugar cube dangling from a piece of string. He's holding it over Putte's snout, teasing him. Every time Putte gets close enough to bite at the cube, the boy snatches it back. Putte yelps unhappily.

"Leave Putte alone!" Stephie tells them.

"Putte," says the boy with the sugar. "Is this mutt named Putte?"

"Putte," repeats Barbro, snorting.

"He's no mutt," Stephie says. "He's pedigreed."

"Ah," says the boy. "A pure canine."

Stephie steps forward to unhook Putte's leash from the hook, but the boy blocks her way. Putte barks and strains at the leash.

"Shush up," Sylvia says, striking Putte hard across the muzzle. Putte whines.

"Don't you dare touch him!" Stephie cries.

"My, my," the other boy, who has been silent until then, says. "She's got some temper."

"Just like the doggie," says the blond one. "Maybe she's pedigreed, too. What do you think?"

Sylvia and Barbro giggle.

"Racially pure," says the freckle-face. "A first-class specimen."

Stephie just wants to get away, but not without Putte.

"Move over," she says to the boy who's blocking her way.

He doesn't move a muscle.

"Did you hear that?" he asked. "Did you hear her tell me to move over? Do we think someone like her can come and tell us Swedes where we can stand?"

"She's the one who should move," says Sylvia, looking at Stephie. "You don't belong here."

"We know why you're here," the freckle-faced boy says. "You people get out of Germany with your money and your jewelry and think you can just buy up our country, like you were trying to do in Germany. But you'll never get away with it. The Germans will be here, too, before you know it, and they'll deal with people like you—you filthy Jew-kid."

For an instant Stephie feels as if she's been turned to stone. Then she flies at the boy, aiming her fist right at his grinning mouth, among all those freckles. She hammers at his chest and kicks at his shins.

The boy is so taken aback, he can't even defend himself. He hadn't expected a girl who would fight. Then he grabs Stephie's wrists and pushes her off him.

"You get away from me," he says, his voice resounding with hate. "Just stay away from me, you make me sick."

A drop of blood is seeping from a crack in his bottom lip.

Putte growls, ears pulled back.

The boy drops Stephie's wrists and shoves her away so hard she tumbles into the gravel. As he pushes her, he takes a step backward. Putte snaps at the boy's trouser leg with his sharp teeth, tearing a big hole in the fabric.

"Ow," the boys shouts. "The mutt bit me!"

He aims a kick at Putte, who howls as the boy's foot strikes him in the ribs.

Stephie throws herself toward Putte. She can't reach the hook on the wall, so she unhooks the leash from his collar.

"Run, Putte!" she shouts. "Run!"

Putte rushes off, a brown-and-white flash along the ground. Stephie gets to her feet and runs after him.

When she comes to the road she stops and turns around. They aren't following her.

"Putte!" she shouts. "Putte, come!"

She can't see him anywhere. Did he run toward home? Or did he just scurry away from his torturers, with no regard for direction?

She sees two little boys playing with a crate on wheels at the edge of the road.

"Have you seen a dog?" she asks them. "Brown and white? Running without a leash?"

"Yup," says one of the little boys. "He went that way," pointing down toward the harbor.

"No," says the other, pointing to the right, toward Britta's. "He went that way."

Stephie wishes she had the bike; then she might catch up with him. But she doesn't dare go back to the shop to get it.

She runs down to the harbor area. No sign of Putte. She

asks the old men sitting on the benches in the sun. None of them has seen a dog off its leash. She turns around and runs back to the intersection where the little boys are playing, then up toward Britta's.

Britta is on her knees in the vegetable patch, weeding.

"Hi," Stephie pants. "Have you seen a dog run by? About ten minutes ago?"

"I just came out," Britta tells her. "What dog?"

Stephie doesn't take the time to answer.

At the end of Britta's road there's a yellow frame house. The lady hanging her washing on the line thinks maybe she did glimpse a dog a few minutes earlier.

"I do think something ran past," she says. "Is it your dog?"

"Yes," Stephie says, so as not to have to go into a long explanation.

"You can cut through our yard," the lady tells her.

Stephie does so, crossing a meadow and jumping a ditch. She takes a wrong step and one of her sandals comes up soaked in wet mud.

"Putte!" she shouts. "Putte!"

She searches for hours, but he's nowhere to be found. Once she thinks she hears him barking behind some juniper bushes, but when she's forced her way through the brambles, he isn't there.

In the end she gives up and collapses onto a rock. She's exhausted from all the running. Her bare legs are covered with scratches.

What is she to do? Putte's lost and it's her fault. Not to mention that she's been in a fight, with a summer guest, of all people, and split his lip. And Putte ruined the guest's trousers, trying to defend her.

Putte's a city dog, not accustomed to fending for himself in the countryside. Maybe he's stuck between rocks, or has broken a leg. It may be ages before someone finds him. He may starve to death. Or be caught by a fox. He may already be dead.

Aunt Märta will be beside herself. She'll make Stephie apologize to all of them—the doctor's wife, Karin, the freckle-faced boy. And Jesus.

No, she'll never apologize to that boy. Not after what he said. She hadn't done anything bad to him. But if she tells them what happened, no one will believe her. It will be four against one, and she knows that both Sylvia and Barbro tell lies.

Anyway, she doesn't want to tell them what the boy said. She doesn't want to tell anyone. She's ashamed. Although nothing that happened was her fault, she's ashamed just the same.

She can't go home.

It's hot enough to spend the night outside. But she'll have to get some food. If she waits until evening, she can sneak into the root cellar at home unseen.

And she still has that package of cookies in her pocket. She can get through the day on cookies. They're all broken and crumbly now. She must have fallen on them when the boy pushed her to the ground. She opens the package and takes out a cookie. She'll save the rest until she's famished.

thirty-eight

How can a day be so long? Hour by hour, the sun shifts from the east of the island to the very top of the sky. Then it continues west, so slowly you can hardly tell.

Now and then Stephie thinks she hears Putte barking, but it's probably just her imagination; at least she never catches sight of him. Her stomach's growling. Occasionally she allows herself a cookie, to stave off the hunger.

It's a hot day. The sun is glaring down and there is hardly so much as a cool breeze. Stephie's thirsty.

She tries to pretend she's shipwrecked on a desert island—a game she played with herself when she first arrived. But a desert island ought to have trees with delicious fruit that fills you up and quenches your thirst. Stephie suddenly remembers the blackberry bramble Vera showed her last summer. But it's only June, and the bushes are just full of white blossoms.

Behind the blackberry bushes there's a crevice in the rocks, dark and deep. The sun can't penetrate there.

Stephie takes a couple of cautious steps down into the crevice. The air is cool and damp. Under her feet there's soft, sandy soil.

She continues farther in and hears the murmur of running water. There's a little rivulet springing up out of the stone, running down the side of the rock. Stephie cups her hands, holding them under the trickle. Then she takes a little sip. The water smells of earth and iron, but it doesn't taste bad.

Just before the other end of the crevice, she discovers a little cave. Inside, the sandy soil is covered with thin green grass. A cool, shady spot.

Stephie lies down. The grass tickles her bare arms and legs. It's very quiet. She can't even hear the ocean in here. The only sound is the persistent chirruping of a grasshopper.

She stays in the cave for a long time. Sleeps for a while, lies awake thinking. Nibbles on cookies, one at a time.

In the end she gets cold. Stiffly, she rises and walks back through the crevice. She splashes her face with water and has another drink. Strangely, she no longer feels hungry, just weak and dizzy.

The sun has begun to sink in the west, down toward the surface of the water. Then it sets so fast, Stephie thinks she can almost see it slip into the water. The sky is cloudless, the pastel colors shifting rapidly from pink to purple to pale blue to green. Just before the sun disappears it is shrouded in a grayish pink haze.

The warmth in the air vanishes in a hurry. Stephie shivers. She's got to get something warm. Perhaps there's an old blanket or sweater in the boathouse.

It's getting dark. The sky is deep blue, except in the west, where there is still a band of light. Aunt Märta must be asleep by now. She goes to bed at ten every night, summer and winter. The summer guests might still be up, but she'll have to take that risk. She's too cold and hungry to wait any longer.

Stephie walks along the beach, approaching the house from below. The white paint looks almost iridescent in the twilight. The windows are all dark except the one in her room upstairs. Sven must be up; he's probably reading in bed. He'll surely never lend her any more books.

The door of the root cellar creaks when she opens it. Quickly she gathers some tins, a jar of jam, and a couple of carrots, putting everything in a paper bag.

Now I'm a real thief, she thinks.

She needs a bottle to fill with water from the pump.

They keep empty bottles and jars on the top shelf. Stephie has to stand on a step stool, and even there she has to stand on tiptoe to reach. Just as she's extending her arm to take a bottle, she loses her balance and grabs the edge of the shelf. It totters and, for a moment, Stephie is sure all the bottles and jars are going to crash to the floor.

But she's lucky. The shelf holds. She takes a bottle and gets down off the stool. Setting the paper bag of provisions outside the root cellar door, she heads for the pump.

As she turns the corner of the yard, Stephie sees to her horror that there's a light on in the basement.

She'll have to pass by the lighted window to reach the pump, and she decides that the best thing to do is to sidle along the wall of the house and crawl under the window, which is only about a yard above the ground.

One step at a time, Stephie creeps to the window and crouches down. But her curiosity gets the better of her and she raises her head just high enough to peek in over the sill.

The light comes from the basement bedroom. Aunt Märta's sitting on the edge of the bed in her nightgown, a long braid hanging down her back. Stephie's never seen her hair in anything but a bun before.

Aunt Märta's head is bowed. It can't be true, but she actually appears to be crying.

Stephie cranes her neck to see better. At that very moment Aunt Märta raises her eyes, and looks right through the window. Stephie ducks as fast as she can, but it's too late.

"Hello?" Aunt Märta cries. "Is anybody there?"

It would still be possible for Stephie to run, grab the bag of provisions, and be out of sight before Aunt Märta got outside.

"It's me," says Stephie, standing up.

Aunt Märta isn't angry. She takes Stephie by the hand, leads her into the basement kitchen, and makes her some sandwiches and cocoa.

"Eat now," she says. "You must be starving."

"I took some food from the root cellar," Stephie whispers. "It's in a bag outside."

"Were you going to run away?" Aunt Märta asks.

Stephie doesn't know how to answer. So much has happened, and she's very tired.

"There were these boys," she begins. "Outside the shop."

"You don't need to tell me," Aunt Märta interrupts. "I know all about it."

A bite of bread catches in Stephie's throat. Somebody's already told Aunt Märta what she did. Was it the shopkeeper? Or the parents of the boys? Of course the doctor's wife must have come down to find out where Putte was. As soon as she has eaten her sandwiches, Aunt Märta will scold her, and tomorrow she'll have to make her apologies.

"Vera returned the bicycle," Aunt Märta says. "Vera Hedberg. She thought you might have run home. She told me the whole story."

"But Putte," Stephie says. "I had to let him go. I think . . . I think he must be dead."

"Dead?" Aunt Märta exclaims. "He's no more dead than I am. He came hobbling home quite early, around ten o'clock. Apparently he injured a paw, but the doctor's wife says he'll be fine."

Stephie can no longer hold back her tears. She rests her head on her arms along the tabletop and sobs.

"I just don't understand you, my girl," Aunt Märta tells her. "Crying because the dog's not dead?"

Stephie hears Aunt Märta's words, but she also hears a different voice. Softer than usual.

"Mimi's dead," Stephie manages to say between gulps.

"Now you blow your nose. Aunt Märta passes her a handkerchief. "And tell me what you're talking about."

So Stephie tells her all about the night when the men with the guns came. The night they took Papa away.

"They banged on the door, and then knocked it down before anyone could open it. There were lots of them, maybe ten. They all had guns, but none of them wore a uniform. A few came into our room. They told us to get up and go out into the hallway. Mamma wanted to give Nellie and me our slippers, but they wouldn't let her.

"We had to line up in the hall," Stephie continues. "Everyone who lived in the apartment: Mamma, Papa, Nellie and me, the Goldbergs and their baby, old Mrs. Silberstein and her blind son, the Reichs and their three children. The floor was freezing cold. One of the men, the one giving the orders, kept marching back and forth in front of us. Every so often he would point his gun at someone."

"I've never heard the like," says Aunt Märta. It sounds as if she is talking to herself, not to Stephie.

"Mimi began to whine," Stephie goes on. "Why couldn't she have kept quiet? I guess their dogs, two huge German shepherds, scared her. 'Oh, so you've got a dog,' one of the men said. 'Don't you know Jew-vermin aren't allowed to have pets?' 'The dog belongs to the children,' Papa said. That was when the man shot her. Mimi fell on her back, legs thrashing. Then she was still. There was blood on the floor. I got some on my foot."

"Dearest child," Aunt Märta says. "My dear little child." She puts a hand atop Stephie's head, stroking her hair. "You go to bed now," she tells her. "Try to get some sleep. We won't let anybody harm you here."

231

thirty-nine

The smell of coffee tingles in Stephie's nose. She opens her eyes. Aunt Märta is standing by the stove pouring coffee into a blue-flowered cup.

"Oh, awake at last," she says. The voice is her usual abrasive one.

It must all have been a dream. It can't be possible that Aunt Märta spoke gently and kindly to her yesterday. Stroked her hair. Stephie must have been dreaming.

"I'm getting up right now," Stephie assures her, sitting up in the trundle bed.

"Do that," Aunt Märta says. "And put on a nice dress. We're going to pay a visit to the shopkeeper's summer guests."

That can only mean one thing: Stephie is going to have to apologize to that freckle-faced boy.

"Do I have to?"

But Aunt Märta's already gone into the other room to make her bed.

Stephie gets dressed and has some bread and butter. She has no appetite, but she forces herself to finish, eating as slowly as she can. Then she combs her hair, as slowly as she can, in front of the mirror.

Aunt Märta's getting impatient. "Won't you be ready soon?"

"Yes," says Stephie. "But I can't find my barrette."

She knows very well where it is: in the pocket of the dress she had on yesterday. Aunt Märta gives her a different one.

"Let's go," she says.

Outside, they find Sven crouching down, scratching Putte's belly. Putte's on his back, kicking his legs. One of his paws is bandaged.

"How is he?" Stephie asks.

"He's all right," Sven tells her. "Nothing's broken, just some swelling. He's going to be fine."

"Come along," Aunt Märta says brusquely. "You can talk about it later."

Stephie sits behind her on the carrier, just like the day she arrived. When they get to the last curve before the shop, Vera appears, jumping off a rock where she's clearly been waiting for them.

Aunt Märta walks the bike the rest of the way.

"Now, Vera," she says. "Have you considered what I said to you?"

Vera nods.

Instead of going into the shop, Aunt Märta opens the gate to the yard. The shopkeeper comes out onto the steps.

"Good morning," he says. "Can I help you?"

"Good morning," Aunt Märta replies. "There's something we need to speak with your summer guests about."

"I see," says the shopkeeper. "Well, I believe they're up."

"I should hope so," Aunt Märta scoffs. "It's not exactly the crack of dawn."

She marches into the yard with Stephie and Vera on her heels. The shopkeeper follows close behind.

The summer guests are sitting outside having their morning meal. Both boys are there, as well as a younger girl, just as freckly as her brother. The man of the family is tall and heavyset, and almost bald. His wife looks much younger, with neatly permed fair hair. There's a young girl in a white apron serving them at the table.

"Excuse me," says the shopkeeper. "There's someone to see you."

"Märta Jansson," Aunt Märta introduces herself. "This is my foster daughter, Stephanie."

"Aha," the bald man says. "And what can we do for you?"

"Can this not wait?" his wife asks, annoyed. "We're at breakfast."

The freckle-faced boy avoids looking at Stephie. He keeps his eyes lowered and seems completely preoccupied with his bowl of oatmeal.

"You finish eating," says Aunt Märta. "We can wait."

Sylvia appears, coming through the back door of the shop. She stops a short distance from the table in the yard, pretending she's weeding a flower bed.

"Go right ahead," says the man. "Speak your piece."

"It concerns one of your sons," says Aunt Märta.

"I see," the man says. "Ragnar, was this the girl?"

"Yes," the boy mumbles, without looking up. His spoon clatters against the bowl.

"We're prepared to let the matter go," says Ragnar's father. "His trousers are ruined, but we're not going to demand compensation. An apology will suffice."

"Perfectly new trousers," the woman adds angrily. "And bloodstains on his shirt. There must be something wrong with that girl!"

"If anyone should apologize," says Aunt Märta very slowly and clearly, "it is certainly not Stephanie."

"I see," the man repeats. "Who do you think ought to, then?"

"Perhaps your son didn't explain why Stephanie hit him?"

"No," his father replies, waving his hand as if Aunt Märta were a bothersome fly he was trying to get rid of.

"Well, let me tell you, then," Aunt Märta goes on. "She hit him because he called her a 'filthy Jew-kid' and said the Germans would soon be here to get her."

The bald man goes bright red. His palm slaps the table-top so hard the coffee cups rattle and the cutlery clatters.

"Is that true?" he asks his son.

"No," the boy says. "She's lying. Isn't she, Gunnar?"

His brother shrugs. "I didn't hear," he replies.

"Is that so?" Aunt Märta asks. "Aren't fine folks like you brought up to tell the truth?"

"Well, it's her word against theirs," the man says. "It may be an excuse your foster daughter invented after the fact."

"Vera," Aunt Märta says, "who's telling the truth? Stephie or that young man?"

Vera almost whispers her answer. "He called her . . . that name. And he kicked Putte."

"Vera came to my house yesterday morning," Aunt Märta tells everyone. "At the time, neither she nor I had yet spoken with Stephie, who was so frightened she was hiding. Vera told me the whole story, and a few other things I didn't know as well. But that," she says, looking meaningfully at Sylvia and the shopkeeper, "will have to be a later matter."

"Ragnar," the man says, "is what the girls and Mrs. Jansson are saying the truth?"

Ragnar nods. "But *you've* said—"

"Not another word!" his father roars.

"No one," says Aunt Märta, "no one is going to come along and say such things to my little girl. I don't care how fine a family he comes from. So Stephie won't be apologizing. But we'll pay for the trousers. How much did they cost?"

The man shakes his head dismissively. His face is as red as a beet.

"There's really no need."

"Nine seventy-five," his wife interjects.

Aunt Märta takes out her wallet, opens it, removes a ten-kronor bill, and sets it on the table.

"Keep the change," she says. "Come along, Stephie."

"My little girl," Aunt Märta had said. My little girl! As if Stephie were her very own child.

forty

Stephie and Vera are lying on the cliff above the swimming cove. Stephie's wearing the red bathing suit Auntie Alma gave her. Vera's wearing her green one. They've just come up out of the water.

They lie close together, on their backs, arms at their sides. The sun has warmed the cliff, and the hot rock is heating their backs. Fanned out behind them and dripping wet are Stephie's long black hair and Vera's bright red hair. Drops of water glisten on their bare skin.

Stephie's never been so tan in her life. "Brown as a ginger snap," Aunt Märta says. Vera doesn't get tan. Early in the summer she was pink; now her fair skin is full of tiny freckles.

"I'll miss you this fall," says Vera. "When you're at

grammar school in town. Though I'm happy for you, of course," she hastens to add.

"I'll miss you, too," says Stephie. "I'll come home for vacations, though, and sometimes even for weekends."

She still can't really believe it's true.

That Uncle Evert and Aunt Märta changed their minds.

It was mainly the doctor's wife's doing, Stephie thinks. When Stephie returned the first pile of books Sven had lent her, the doctor's wife was the only one at home. She invited Stephie in to sit down, and they talked about the books and about school.

A few days later the doctor's wife invited Aunt Märta and Stephie in for coffee. Aunt Märta had to be asked twice, but in the end, she gave in.

The doctor's wife told Aunt Märta she considered Stephie a gifted girl, one who ought to be allowed to continue her schooling. Aunt Märta replied she knew that very well, but they couldn't afford to board her in town, not to mention all the other expenses.

That was when the doctor's wife explained that after Karin and her fiancé got married at the end of August there would be an empty bedroom in the family's apartment in Göteborg. They just happened to live very close by the girls' grammar school, and Stephie was welcome to lodge in the room. She wouldn't have to pay for anything but her meals. There were grants they could apply for, too, to cover the cost of books and other school supplies.

Aunt Märta thanked the doctor's wife and asked if she could think the matter over. She wanted to talk to Evert about it when he came back from his fishing trip.

All the next week, Stephie went out of her way to be even nicer and more helpful than usual. She didn't know whether that was what clinched it, but in the end Aunt Märta and Uncle Evert said yes.

The doctor's wife promised to arrange for Stephie to be registered at the girls' grammar school, even though it was already past the deadline. The headmistress was a friend of hers. Miss Bergström lent Stephie the math book again. Stephie had to work on her own, but Miss Bergström promised to help her if she got stuck.

"What if you and Sylvia end up in the same class again?" Vera asks.

"That won't bother me at all," Stephie replies.

She isn't bragging. Ever since that morning in the shopkeeper's yard, she's felt that Sylvia can do her no harm.

"No, I guess she won't rule the roost at the grammar school, anyway," Vera says. She's quiet for a few minutes, before adding softly, "And in town you'll make new friends. City girls."

"Right," says Stephie. "I hope so. But you're my best friend, whatever happens."

When she hears herself say that, she feels a tweak at her heart. It's been weeks since she wrote to Evi.

"You and Evi," she adds quickly.

"Who's Evi?"

"My best friend in Vienna. We met in first grade. We always sat next to each other in class."

"Do you miss her?

"Mmm, sometimes."

"And your parents?"

239

"Oh, yes."

"I miss my father," Vera tells her.

Vera's father is dead. He drowned before Vera was born. He and Vera's mother hadn't even gotten married yet.

"It's really strange to think about Mamma and Papa and Evi and all the other people back at home," Stephie says. "To imagine them walking on the same old streets, while I'm here."

"Would you rather be there?"

"I'd rather they were here."

"Couldn't they come?"

"I'm not sure. The doctor's wife has promised to write to someone who might be able to help us."

Stephie shuts her eyes tight. In the bright sunlight, the blood vessels on the inside of her eyelids shimmer. It's very hot. She sits up.

"Come on, let's have a swim," she says.

The water is crystal clear. You can see straight down to the bottom. Dark green strips of seaweed bobble at the water's edge. Stephie picks one up, pushing on the yellowish bubbles till they burst with a popping sound. The seaweed is known as bladder kelp, but the children call it bubble kelp.

"Dip or dive?" Vera asks.

"Dive," says Stephie.

They climb up the diving rock and gaze out over the surface of the water. You have to be careful not to land right on a stinging jellyfish. Stephie had bad luck once, and got red hives all over her chest and arms.

They see one big orange one floating a couple of yards from their diving rock.

"We'll have to jump left," Vera says. "They have such long tentacles."

"I'll go first," says Stephie, taking a deep breath and holding her nose. Taking a running jump, she splashes into the water.

Eyes open, she sinks into the shimmering green depths. For an instant her body hovers, weightless. Then she comes panting up to the surface, just in time to see Vera plunge from the rock.

It's been a hot summer. Now that it's August, the water's so warm you can stay in as long as you like and not get cold.

They take turns diving for stones on the bottom. As they're clambering up over the rocks to get out, Stephie scrapes one knee on a barnacle, a sharp-edged shell that attaches to the rocks, just below the surface.

Her knee bleeds a little. Stephie examines her legs, covered with bruises, scrapes, and scratched-open mosquito bites. The skin on the bottoms of her feet has grown thick and hard from walking barefoot.

She's different now from the girl she was a year ago, when she arrived on the island. It shows.

Stephie and Vera lie in the sun to dry, then put on their clothes. There's a thin layer of salt from the water on Stephie's tan skin. She licks one of her arms for the salty taste.

Nellie and Sonja are splashing in the water at the shore.

"Hey, Stephie," Nellie shouts. "Watch me swim!"

Nellie's just learned; she can do both the crawl and the breaststroke. She tumbles in the water like a chubby dolphin.

Stephie's and Vera's bikes are parked just above the beach. Stephie's gleams red in the sun, as shiny as it was when she got it a few weeks ago for her thirteenth birthday. It was standing outside the basement door when she woke up in the morning. Her very own bicycle.

When they reach the main road, Vera asks, "Is it all right if I come home with you? We can rinse each other's hair under the pump."

"Sure," Stephie replies.

They bike on the path that leads through the thicket and up the long hill. Stephie stops at the top.

"What's the matter?" Vera wonders. "It's all downhill from here."

Stephie doesn't answer. She stares out across the ocean, to where the sky and water meet in the west. Somewhere beyond the horizon there's more land. Next year, on Easter Eve, there will be bonfires on islands she can't see today, although the weather is beautiful. The islands are out there, and so is the mainland.

America is there, too, a mirage on the other side of the Atlantic. Norway, however, occupied by the Germans, is much too near. Vienna, where Mamma, Papa, and Evi are, is much too far away. Aunt Märta is in the white house at the bottom of the hill, along with Uncle Evert, the doctor's wife, and Sven. Beside her, there's Vera.

Stephie's not at the end of the world. She's on a faraway island, but she is not alone.

"Come on," she says to Vera. "Last one down the hill's a rotten egg!"

author's note

$\mathcal{I}$ was born into a Jewish family in Göteborg, on the west coast of Sweden, nearly sixty years ago. Early on I understood how fortunate I was that my parents had grown up in Sweden—and not in Germany (where my mother was born), or in Belarus (from where my grandparents on my father's side fled to Sweden in the early 1900s), or in Austria or Holland or France or even Norway: had they spent World War II in any of those places, they would probably not have survived the war. I might never have been born at all.

As a child I used to look through my mother's photo album. There were pictures of relatives I had never met, including her father's grandparents, aunts, uncles, and cousins. Some of them were living in the United States, Israel, or Brazil; others had perished during the war. Nobody would tell me how they had died, but of course it wasn't long until I understood.

I didn't have much extended family in Sweden on my mother's side, only her two cousins, who were about her age and had come to Sweden all alone, thanks to my grandfather's efforts; his business had brought him to Göteborg as early as the 1920s.

My mother's cousins were among the few Jewish refugees from Nazi Germany who were granted asylum in Sweden. Like so many other countries, Sweden at first closed its borders to the hundreds of thousands of German and Austrian Jews lining up outside embassies and consulates to obtain an entry visa to another country. But after Kristallnacht in November 1938, when the Nazis burned down so many synagogues, pillaged and vandalized Jewish shops, and rounded up thousands of people for deportation to concentration camps, the small Jewish congregations in Sweden pleaded with the government and managed to arrange for five hundred children from Germany, Austria, and Czechoslovakia to be brought to Sweden. Adult Jews, however, were still to be kept out of the country.

Five hundred children. Not a large number compared to the ten thousand Jewish children who got to England at the same time, thanks to the Kindertransport, or "children's transports." Really not a large number compared with the seventy thousand Finnish children who were evacuated to Sweden only a year later, when the Soviet Union attacked Finland. And virtually a negligible number in comparison with the millions who would shortly be put to death in the concentration camps.

Still, some children were saved. Five hundred children and young people were brought to Sweden from Berlin and Hamburg, Vienna and Prague. Half of them were young teenagers, and around fifteen percent were children under the age of seven, with some as young as one year old. The average age was twelve, and almost two-thirds were girls. They left their parents behind, as well as any siblings too young or too old to be taken. They also left behind all their relatives, friends, and classmates, even their pets. Although some had a brother, sister, or friend with them on the train, most came alone.

The majority of these five hundred children came from urban areas and middle-class families, where a strong tradition of education existed. In Sweden, however, these boys and girls often ended up living in rural areas, where it was far from a given that they would attend school for more than the compulsory six years. Once these refugee children reached age thirteen or so, they tended to be taken advantage of as unpaid farmhands and housemaids. Sadly, even when the children were placed with Jewish families, as a small number of them were, it did not guarantee that they received any better treatment. The only advantage was that they, at least, were able to continue practicing their religion. Others, like Stephie and Nellie in *A Faraway Island*, found themselves in strict Christian homes, where their foster parents were eager to get them to embrace Jesus in their hearts.

The refugee children arrived in Sweden believing that they would soon be reunited with their families, but when the war finally ended, several years later, only about one in four of them had even one parent who had survived. Those who were able to be reunited with a parent or relative emigrated from Sweden, often to the United States, Canada, or Israel. More than half of the five hundred children, however, ended up spending the rest of their lives in Sweden. In spite of their difficult experiences, most of them managed to get an education and a job and to have a family. Many married young, perhaps hoping to create new families after having lost their original ones. Some became very successful professionals.

One thing nearly all of them had in common was that after the war there were many years when they barely spoke of their experiences, of the separation from their parents or the difficulty of being refugee children. The pain was so great, it had to be suppressed. Some of them never even told their own children where they had come from, or why. Not until fifty years after their escape did many begin to feel that the time had come to tell their tales, before it was too late. I am deeply grateful to those who were willing to share their experiences with me.

A *Faraway Island* is the first of four novels I have written about Stephie and Nellie. These novels are based on interviews with about a dozen of the real refugees who shared their childhoods, their letters, and their diaries, as well as on the research of Ingrid Lomfors, a Jewish historian in Sweden who explored the destinies of the five hundred refugee children. I have also listened to my own parents' stories about what it was like to live as Jewish teenagers in Sweden during World War II. I made journeys myself, to Vienna and to the Theresienstadt concentration camp near

Prague, to gather my own impressions. Some of the events in the books are real, others are what might have been. Stephie and Nellie are fictional characters, but I have borrowed elements of real human beings in creating them—including myself and my nearest and dearest.

Early in the process of writing these books, I decided against writing in the first person, feeling that stories in the "I" form should be told by the people who really had the firsthand experience—the Holocaust survivors. My books are, therefore, written in the third person, but with a focus on Stephie's thoughts and feelings. *A Faraway Island* is, though, in the present tense. This was also a conscious decision. I didn't want to tell Stephie's story as historical, but as a story in the here and now. Today, too, children and young people have to escape from their countries, leaving their families behind. And even today, the care we give to refugee children who arrive alone, in Sweden and other wealthy nations, is not what it ought to be. One of my aspirations for these books about Stephie and Nellie is that they will contribute to a better understanding of the vulnerable situation in which refugee children continue to live.

about the author

ANNIKA THOR was born and raised in a Jewish family in Göteborg, Sweden. She has been a librarian, has written for both film and theater, and is the author of many books for children and young adults. She lives in Stockholm.

A *Faraway Island* is the first of four novels featuring the Steiner sisters. The quartet has been translated into numerous languages and has garnered awards worldwide. Swedish television also adapted the books into a hugely popular eight-part series.